A FLIGHTLESS
BIRD

GYENI GOMAN

Conscious Dreams
PUBLISHING

A FLIGHTLESS BIRD

Copyright © 2024: Gyeni Goman

Published by Conscious Dreams Publishing
www.consciousdreamspublishing.com

Mentored by Daniella Blechner
Edited by Daniella Blechner and Elise Abram
Typeset and ebook formatting by: Amit Dey
Cover Designed by Emily's World of Design

ISBN: 978-1-915522-98-6

TABLE OF CONTENTS

ACKNOWLEDGEMENTS

I first started working on this book when I was 10 years old and over the years, I have continued to revisit it and develop it into what you see today.

A huge thanks firstly goes to Daniella Blechner and all at Conscious Dreams Publishing for supporting me, guiding me and ultimately getting this book over the finish line. Completing this book has been a long process, and she has been very patient with me and mentored me through the whole process.

Thank you to Madison for being a good friend over all these years and for bringing a smile to my face during challenging times.

I would like to thank my supportive family - the Testers, the Agyapongs and Willmott. They continue to believe in me and they are my biggest cheerleaders.

Special thanks goes out to my amazing nan, Denise. She is a rock and always looks out for me.

I would like to thank my older brother Malachi for helping design this book cover and for putting up with me, the 'favourite' child. I also can't forget my younger brother, Xander, for all his energy and joy. Thank you to my cats, Spike, Twilight and Custard, for giving me the emotional support I need!

Lastly, I would like to give thanks to my mum and dad. Since I was young, you have encouraged my storytelling and drawing, giving me the space to create and imagine new worlds and characters. Even though I can drive you insane at times, I want you to know that I have nothing but love for you both. Thank you.

PART ONE

LIVING
WHILE DYING

1

I gasped, my lungs desperate for air. Mucus stuck in my throat, stiff and salty. Perspiration ran down my back. I blinked twice and then once more, trying to clear the white fog from the corners of my eyes. I sat up, rigid with fear and some trace of anger. My heart jumped from my chest into my throat, caught in the build-up of bile like a fly in a web.

The nightmare that woke me was slipping away, leaving only fragments of the bigger picture behind.

'It's okay,' I told myself, clutching my sweaty, bare arms. 'She doesn't hate you.' I exhaled, relaxing my chest. 'It's fine.'

A gust of strong wind blew back my pleated grey curtains, letting a sliver of the shy, dim, red moonlight crawl in to invade my room like vermin hatching in a pristine pond. It irradiated the empty space I had tried to cover up with bookcases full of novels I'd probably never get around to reading, the shelves of glistening crystals and plants trapped in resin, the posters and picture frames holding nothing in particular, and trophy upon trophy that tried to fill the room. They all stared back at me, looking sinister in the dark.

I've digested the memory.

I've swallowed my guilt.

Nothing, and I mean *nothing*, could ever take her place.

Samantha.

She'd always be there, behind the bookcases, beneath the pretty floral wallpaper, always there, always watching. The marks her bed had left on the walls had to be erased. Her awards had to be hidden. No one would know—no one had to know—that she had ever been there. It was almost as if we were trying to forget her, like if there were no trace of her, the pain wasn't real.

Like my sister wasn't real.

I couldn't just sit there and play the victim—I was the perpetrator.

I'd bought the new furniture, ripped down the posters, painted the walls and thrown out her things. It was all an insult to her memory, a memory that almost didn't exist.

I remember when I felt normal, when I felt like a person and not just a clump of cells and electrons floating around in condensed form, tethered to the earth by nothing more than gravity and fear.

Que sera, sera, I guess. Whatever that means.

2

I think the sun rose sometime around six, but by then, I was already stuck standing at the bus stop, the rain pelting down on me.

The bus stop wasn't actually a bus stop. It was just a sign in the ground, the post bent backwards and forwards every which way. It meant I was soaked, tortured and chilled by the moody October weather while innocently waiting for the school bus, scheduled to arrive at six minutes past seven.

Thank *God* the half-term was near.

The wind whistled in my ears, barely audible over the sound of my teeth chattering and my knees knocking.

I checked my watch.

7:04 AM

I stared at the numbers for what felt like two full minutes. It's funny how time moves, or rather, how my perception of it functions. When I take notice of it, time moves like a slug as opposed to when I forsake it or when I'm late.

The clouds clumped together in pink blobs of cumulus and peachy altostratus, surrounding the golden drops of sunlight shining through the thick trees on the other side of the road. The pavement beneath my feet was peppered with gross feathers, dry bird droppings, squashed blackberries and litter so old it had been compressed into the concrete by people walking upon it. Surprisingly, the amalgam of modern nature didn't stink. In fact, I couldn't smell anything at all. My lack of smell may have been due to my shifting senses, the fact that it was freezing cold, or that I cut a twenty-minute walk into a five-minute jog, but who knows?

I pulled out my bus pass in anticipation, fumbling with frozen fingers.

As I took off my bag, I heard the groan of tyres coming around the corner, and I checked my watch once again.

7:05 AM

'Early, for once,' I murmured.

I ran up the steps to board the school bus, conscious of the people behind me, briefly flashing my bus pass at the driver. As per usual, I travelled to the back, prepared to occupy my seat by the window, but it was taken.

The girl with large, glassy eyes the colour of faded pistachios was not someone I'd seen before. Her silky-looking hair fell to her collarbone in coils of brown-streaked auburn. Freckles outlined her siren eyes. Her eyelid was bruised to the point where it had inherited a yellowish tinge. Red, mottled skin formed around her hooked nose and peach-like lips, barely noticeable against her almond-brown skin.

She smiled at me. It was the smile of somebody who'd been to hell and back but still looked at the world as if it were a lovely thing.

I stopped in my tracks and gawped at her like a moron, forgetting about finding a seat for the moment, focusing on the burning hatred I felt behind my eyes.

I held my tongue and sat on the seat parallel to my normal one.

'Hey.' I heard a voice.

I went to place my hand on the armrest and recoiled when I remembered it was the one usually covered in chewing gum.

'Hey!' somebody whispered, but I ignored it because it was unlikely they were calling me.

Leaning my head on the window, I opened my bag to get out my iPod. As I plugged in my headphones, something jagged and white collided with the side of my head, a piece of screwed-up paper.

I looked in the direction from whence it came and saw a dark-eyed girl with a jotter sitting open on her lap. She shuffled over to the aisle seat to come closer to me. 'Open it,' she mouthed.

I unfolded the crinkled piece of paper.

I DIDN'T DO THE ~~SIENCE~~ SCIENCE HOMEWORK!!!

I looked back at her. 'Well, what do you want me to do about it?'

'Gimme yours.' She stood up, gripping the back of her seat as if it were her only lifeline.

'Val-Valerie, sit down. It's not due until tomorrow.'

Ignoring my request, Valerie did not sit down. 'Come on! If you do mine, I'll buy you a pack of Haribos, I swear,' Val said in a voice that was supposed to be appealing but made me gag.

'I was going to do it before you said that. Anyway, Sir knows my handwriting.'

She reached for my bag with feline-like claws.

'Get your grotty fingers away from me!' I screeched, causing several heads to turn.

'Can I just copy it?'

'Fifty pence on the spot.' I huffed, still winded from the scream.

'I don't have my purse,' she whined and flicked her long, fair hair over her shoulder.

'Tough.'

'I'll give you my blood,' she pleaded.

I looked over at her in disgust. 'I want cash. I can't buy my Pick n' Mix with blood.'

'Umm…you know what? Fine.' Reluctantly, Valerie pulled out her bus wallet and handed me a one-pound coin.

'Thought you didn't have your purse with you.'

'I thought you could be swayed.'

After unzipping my bag, I pulled out my green science book and passed it diagonally to my friend.

'Stingy cow,' she said.

'Happy to help.'

The rest of the bus trip transpired in silence…or relative silence. I listened to my downloaded music, Valerie copied my homework, the new girl enjoyed her stolen seat, and the bus driver tried to kill us all with his probably illegal, drunk driver-esque turns.

It was all normal, with only one or two things out of the ordinary.

However, as many know, life turns ordinary on its head. The universe has a hand in everything, and it can change people's lives with a simple encounter or two. I just didn't think anything special, anything big, would ever happen to me.

God, was I stupid or just wilfully ignorant?

8:45 AM

'*Bonjour*, class FR3!' my French teacher said with unreciprocated enthusiasm as she walked into the room in her greasy pink high heels. The class of twenty-four stood, and all chatter was expected to stop from that point forward.

She was met with groans and mumbled words. However, that did not sway her. She stood in front of the whiteboard, gazing at us expectantly with her beady, black eyes.

'*Bonjour, Mademoiselle Wallace*,' the class echoed in a sluggish moan with a sloppy, broken accent. I just mouthed what I was supposed to say—foreign languages weren't my strong suit.

Moodily, I swung my bag onto my desk with enough force to bring down the building. After unzipping it carefully, I grabbed my pencil case, French book and a soaked sheet of paper that was supposed to be my homework and set it all down in front of me, waiting patiently for Miss Wallace to say something foreign.

'*Asseyez-vous, classe.*'

The siren-like bell screamed to declare it was lesson time.

I took my seat and pushed my bag off the three-legged table. Our French room was one of the more neglected classrooms. It often smelled like mildew or dampness. There were ladybugs in the corners of the window frames and mysterious stains on the rotting threadbare carpet. OFSTED gave us an 'outstanding', but that was because they didn't see the FL block. If they had, I doubt our rating would have been higher than 'needs improvement'.

'*Bonjour*, Lily Abrams.'

'*Bonjour, Mademoiselle.*'

I looked to my left. Marcus, an acquaintance of mine, was absent from his seat, which was strange because I'd seen him during tutor time.

Miss Wallace continued registration.

'*Bonjour*, Alex Grace.'

'*Bonjour.*'

My eyes flitted around the classroom, surveying each table. Every desk held three chairs. So far, eight desks out of the nine in the class were full. I felt everyone's eyes on me, making indents in my skin. The room of people I'd known for at least two years suddenly felt so unfamiliar, as if this was something new and frightening.

That was when the door burst open, sending the doorstopper flying across the room.

I exhaled with relief as everybody turned around. I hadn't realised I was holding my breath.

Our head of year, Mr Acharya, popped his head in through the doorway, and Miss Wallace stopped the register. 'Am I interrupting anything?' he asked.

'No, not at—' Miss Wallace started, no doubt secretly quite mad at being interrupted.

'Perfect.'

Our French teacher turned almost purple with rage. She let out a small hissing sound, quite like a kettle, and smiled pleasantly once she had reset herself.

'We have a new pupil starting today. I think they're already on the registration system.'

'Umm...Owens...Ga...Galath?' Miss Wallace retrieved her glasses and squinted at her wide -screen computer with the lenses set lopsided on her taut face.

'That's the one.' Our head of year turned away for a second, whispering quite loudly to somebody in the wings, 'Do you think you could go in there and introduce yourself?'

There didn't seem to be a response. Obviously, his question was rhetorical.

Miss Wallace shook her head frantically as Mr Acharya directed a tall, knock-kneed student into the classroom, reassuring her all the while. You could tell she was new. I could practically smell it on her—the discreet makeup, appropriate-length skirt, pristine collar, perfect, thoroughly brushed hair, unstained blazer, and most of all, the excessive perfume. The Hathem (my school) logo was perfectly stitched onto what was obviously a Primark backpack.

Due to her lateness and lack of recognition of anybody in the room, I made the following assumptions:

1. She had got lost sometime between 8:15 and 8:40.

2. Mr Acharya had already given her a brief tour of the school.

Her hands trembled, and her back was hunched in the most closed position I had ever seen.

Miss Wallace sharply reminded her to tie up her hair, and as a result, received a disapproving glare from Sir.

The new girl tied her tawny hair while glimpsing at the room around her.

Meanwhile, I played with my compass until I felt her gaze resting on me.. Nothing about the girl struck me as special (partially because I couldn't care less about somebody disrupting the friendship dynamic or whatever in the classroom), but that was before I saw her eyes. They were the same washed-out pistachio eyes that had met mine on the bus more than an hour before. Suddenly, my unjustified hatred—prejudice, if you must—returned, boiling the space behind my eyes.

I felt as if I were about to cry.

'*Je m'appelle Galatea Owens, et je suis très heureuse de faire partie de cettecommunauté. J'espère que vous m'accueillirez tous malgré mon arrivée tardive*[1] she said to the French teacher, who became swollen with glee in a very swift mood swing, probably because she didn't have to catch up the new pupil, whose accent was perfect.

'What?' I blurted out when she had finished.

A few heads turned to look at me and shrugged, each of them as clueless as I.

---

[1] Direct translation: I am called Galatea Owens and I am very happy to be a part of this community. I hope you will all welcome me despite my late arrival.

'*Bienvenue*, Galatea!' Miss Wallace laughed, happy for the first time that year.

The new girl nodded and bowed.

The entire class groaned, and my hatred was no longer unjustified—Galatea Owens was under my skin.

Galatea smiled and then frowned as if confused at why everyone seemed so upset.

'You may take your seat next to Mr Ostrovsky at the back there,' Miss Wallace vaguely gestured at me. 'Samson, *levez la main*?'

I stuck my limp hand in the air as I was told and flopped it around haphazardly, like a rubber chicken.

Our teacher's brief spell of happiness seemed to fade with the silence.

Galatea made her way over to me, her oversized uniform rubbing against the tables, sounding like sandpaper. All eyes were on her as she pulled up a chair and took her seat next to me.

'I trust—' Miss Wallace commenced, long, amphibian lips drawn tightly in a sarcastic smile as the head-of-year interrupted her yet again.

'I trust you will all make her feel welcome in the Hathem community. Toodles!' He waved at us and hurried off through the doorway.

Looking rather reptilian with her wrinkled neck stretched to its limit, Miss Wallace poked her head out the door to check that Sir had actually gone. She turned back to the class and sighed as if the weight of the world were on her shoulders. 'Finally, I may speak freely.' She inhaled deeply and resumed the register.

'*Bonjour*, Darcy Johann.'

'*Bonjour, Mademoiselle.*'

Galatea unzipped her cheap backpack and shook the hair out of her eyes in a way that was meant to catch my attention. Rather than acknowledge her, I opened my exercise book and wrote the date in French: *Vendredi 21 Octobre 2005.*

I felt my toes cramp up as I highlighted the date in pastel pink.

'*Bonjour*, Fraiser.'

'*Oui, Mademoiselle.*'

'*Bonjour*, Harriet.'

'*Oui, Mademoiselle.*'

'*Bonjour*, Curtis.'

'*Bonjour.*'

'*Bonjour*, Samson.'

'*Oui, Mademoiselle,*' I answered without a moment's hesitation.

I looked over to Galatea, who was drawing on her fingernails, and grimaced, showing my dislike for her.

'*Bonjour*, Galatea.'

'*Bonjour, Mademoiselle.*'

A semi-forgotten thought resurfaced in my head—where was Marcus?

I leant forward to poke Curtis, the boy in front of me. 'Curt, Curt,' I whispered, my hands on the table as I pressed my chest against my book.

He turned around, rolled his eyes at me, and smiled. 'What do you need?' He mumbled so he wouldn't be heard by people outside of a one-metre radius.

'Do you know where Marc—'

'Shhh!' he silenced me abruptly.

'What?'

'Speak of the devil, and he shall appear,' Curt whispered, waving his hands about in a mystical way, 'Besides, Miss's already in a bad mood. I think it's better he chose to bunk off.'

I gasped, offended by proxy.

He turned back around, so I thought the conversation had ended.

Without blinking, I retreated back into my musty patch of stagnant air. The dead cells, dust particles and varying degrees of bacteria caught in my throat in clumps so thick they were tangible.

The rest of the lesson passed uneventfully. Break and lunch weren't really worth mentioning. I bought my usual from the canteen and sat with the type of friends who would mask my silence, friends like Valerie, who had enough to say for the both of us.

I noticed Galatea at both intervals, sitting near but not next to me. She didn't eat much, just one half of a crustless cheese sandwich and what might have been a granola bar at break. New students are usually flocked with sudden friends, but she seemed to run away from them. More attracted to my presence, she seemed to hover around me as if she were waiting for something.

Weirdo.

Fortunately, time flew by, leaving me free to go where I'd been meaning to visit, somewhere I couldn't bear to go before.

Not home.

Not yet.

3

I said goodbye to my classmates and walked in the exact opposite direction of the bus stop. Going by my slightly unreliable memory, my destination was a ten-minute walk away. Somehow, my feet never grew weary of the walk. I guess it might have something to do with the importance of the infrequent journey.

I took my iPod out from my inner blazer pocket, inserted my headphones into the water-damaged hole, and pressed play on my downloaded mix. My playlist was composed of mostly white noise, video game soundtracks and idle music, in that order.

I thought about pressing the shuffle button, but my blood ran cold with the very idea of disrupting the order in which the music was arranged. Brushing away the silly suggestion, I relaxed my body and submerged myself in the unceasing noise of the current 'song'.

The track I was listening to was reminiscent of when spring turned into summer, with the yellowing grass, glistening rivers and beautiful baby blue nights sprayed with magenta hints of dissipating clouds. It was like the sound of wheat swaying in the wind, different, but only slightly so.

Pollen dusted my eyelashes. My bones creaked inside of me as if my endoskeleton were a badly oiled machine. I closed my tired eyes, letting the music fill me with emotions I would never experience otherwise, trusting my feet to keep me on the straight path. I exhaled and let the darkness comfort me.

For a minute, I lost myself in a sea of everything…and nothing, if that's even possible. The weight was lifted from my chest. I felt happy—maybe even well—for the first time in months until I opened my eyes at the crossroads, and all the evil I'd ever known came flooding back to me in an instant.

I stopped dead in my tracks and let the cold air wash over me. Maybe I should just go home. Then I remembered why I was going.

I took a right at the junction.

Not far now.

The only things I heard were the sound of my footsteps and the music in my ears. This was all just an overture, unimportant and unessential, but still something I had to account for.

The chime of the church bell came late. My hand was on the rusty gate. I looked down at my school shoes, covered in autumn leaves.

Finally there.

About to see *her.*

I entered the sacred place, unintimidated by the weeping angels above the gate.

Rows upon and rows of headstones stuck out of the ground like aberrations in the soil. I roamed the cemetery, skimming the plaques.

It didn't take long for me to find her gravestone—it was the one covered with white chrysanthemums, crimson roses and golden marigolds.

I pressed pause on my music, put my iPod back inside my blazer, and bent down to sit beside the grave.

I checked my watch: 3:15 PM

Close enough.

'Is now a good time?' I whispered to the settled earth beneath my feet, 'Did I miss my chance when I skipped the funeral?'

There was no response, of course, nothing but the clicking of my knees, the chirping of the birds and the bacteria squirming inside me.

Was that weird?

I paused, trying not to swallow my words. 'I just didn't want to see you, not like that, not dead. I mean, you've got to understand that... that it could have been me,' I scoff, feeling the weight of her silence, 'And...in a coffin, even a closed one, you'd seem even more dead than now.'

I leaned my head against the polished headstone.

Even when they pulled her out of the water with the nibbled, bloodstained eyeballs and mottled skin, I could still kid myself that she'd wake up, that someday, the water in her lungs would aid her instead of plague her, but they lost her body and buried nothing but an empty casket.

I was just talking to the idea of her.

'I should have bought you some roses. Maybe that'd make everything better.' I let my legs go limp as I traced my fingers over the words inscribed on her grave.

SAMANTHA MARIAM OSTROVSKY
Beloved by most, missed by all.
1991 - 2004

I grew more and more despondent with each passing second. My chest was bloated with everything I should have said, bloated with tears I couldn't hold in for much longer. They threatened to pour silently out of me…or as silently as grieving tears can.

'Is this…is this how I'm supposed to feel, day and night?'

No answer. What was I expecting, talking to a *grave*?

'I want to die, Saffy, and I… I don't know what to do. If you were here…'

If you cared, you would be here.

Obviously, I didn't voice that last part. If I said it aloud, it would be too true, too real to deny.

'You deserved it.' I coughed and shivered. The wind blew straight through my disgusting body.

'I guess the guilt got the better of me. I almost forgot why I hated you. I almost forgot about him.'

The gate creaked open.

Nonononononononononononoonononoonononononononono!

My body trembled at the thought of being found in this state, but no matter how hard I tried, I couldn't stop crying. My legs didn't work anymore, and I was left hugging the gravestone for stability.

'Are you okay?' The voice wasn't elderly. Or young and pre-pubescent. It wasn't adult-ish, either.

It was an adolescent, probably fresh out of school.

Like me.

Hathem is the only secondary school for five miles. They didn't sound old enough to be in year ten or eleven and not young enough to be in year seven, either.

I saw a flash of glistening copper hair. Only one other person had hair like that, but he was gone.

It couldn't be.

And it wasn't.

So who?

It was Galatea.

The ire resting in the pit of my stomach came alive like a dying fire fed dry wood.

It gave me the strength to stand. 'I...No!' My voice was shaky from the crying, but it sounded firm and full of unfettered rage. I wiped my eyes, feeling my fragile eyelashes, abrasive as they brushed against my hand. I stared at Galatea, hoping my eyes would burn holes in her head. 'I mean, unless you have something to say, some respects to pay, get out.'

She began, her eyes darting around frantically. 'You looked so—'

'I don't care how I looked. You just need to leave.'

'I don't really have any—'

'Go.'

I began moving toward the gate, and she took a few steps back, fear smeared across her face like cheap concealer.

God! She thought...

She thought I could...

Damn.

'Have you been following me?'

'I heard you. Everything. And if you want somebody to talk—'

'You did?' I asked although it was obvious from the way she looked at me from the start: she thought I was crazy, too.

All of the anger fell away from my voice when next I spoke. 'I'm sorry,' I said with a cough.

She stretched out her hand to pat my shoulder tenderly in a way that was unfit for an almost stranger. Her hand made contact with my shoulder, and I flinched from her touch. Galatea pretended not to notice.

'I can't go home like this,' I confessed.

'I'm in a bit of hot water in that area, too. Maybe we could...' A hopeful twinkle appeared in her eyes.

'Do what—the art homework? Come on, let's be honest here: the only thing we have in common are the six assignments we were given today. We keep ourselves to ourselves, as you and I established throughout the school day.' My voiced thoughts hung in the air, but my heart wasn't really in it, and to be honest, I wasn't hell bent on spending any more time in a field full of bones and maggots.

'But I could know you, and you could know me. Maybe if we went into town, bought something to make you feel better (or kill time in my case), and talked, we could try,' she persuaded me, face glowing with hope and all that was good in the world.

She didn't give me any good reason, but like I said, I didn't feel like being stubborn.

'Can you pay?' I asked.

'Sure.'

4

We walked quite a way before my accomplice spotted a phone box, something I didn't know we'd been looking for.

She smacked her forehead with the heel of her hand. 'I have to call my parents,' she said.

'Do you have a mobile?' she asked me, fumbling around in her purse for a twenty-pence coin.

'No, why?'

She stared at me blankly. 'Well, why do you think?'

I didn't answer.

She pulled out a coin, stepped into the phone box, and ushered me in, for some reason. Galatea inserted the coin and skittishly tapped in her home phone number.

It was 7-7-something-1-0-something-5-9- something-something.

The greasy, black telephone rang for about five seconds before somebody picked up.

'Hello, this is the Torres residence,' said a small voice from the speaker.

'It's Galatea,' she answered, voice pretentiously sweet. 'So...anyway...Mummy,' Galatea continued, 'I'm coming home around half past five.'

'No, you're not,' the voice replied.

'Yes...I am. That's what I'm telling you.'

'Galatea Eleanor Owens, I swear to God, if you come home any later than half past four—'

'You're not going to do anything. If you do, Charis is gonna report you. Anyhow, I'm going now, 'cause the call's almost over and—oh, bye.' She hung up in the middle of her own sentence and rolled her eyes.

'Hate her,' She exhaled as we walked out of the stuffy phone booth and strolled down the path ahead of me.

'You can't. She's your mum.'

'Not biologically. Or adoptively,' my acquaintance answered rather vaguely.

'Like, she's a step or foster parent?'

'Foster. Her name's Coral... I think. I know she won't last long,' she said wistfully.

'What do you mean?' I asked, way too invested in this girl's life.

She turned to me, walking backwards now. 'I've been through a few foster parents. They were nice, but I ruined them. I'd do all kinds of things, stupid things, and then they'd mess up in turn, screaming at me or throwing something. My social worker would be called, and I'd be off to somebody new. I've moved all over, seen everything and everyone. Nothing differs. There are just new faces with the same names and the same bland stories. They all think they're so special, so unique, when nothing has changed.'

She paused, standing still for a moment, maybe regretting her confession.

'Come on—I know a shortcut to the bakery!' Galatea rushed off into a tall thicket around the farmland area. I speed-walked behind her, unable to run due to my general unfitness.

Following a stranger? And a dangerous one at that, said a voice inside my head. *My, my, I thought you'd got smarter.* The rational part of my brain jeered at me, awakening from its year-long slumber.

It's fine. I know her, I told it.

No, you don't, it answered. *You met her properly like an hour ago—how can you know she won't exploit you?*

I just do, okay?

This is how Dean Corll lured his victims in.

This isn't Texas, I growled at it. And besides, I know her from school.

I crinkled through the possumwood leaves, orange debris getting stuck in the ridges of my shoes.

If you say so, my conscience said before disappearing, leaving me alone again.

Completely alone with that girl up in front of me, camouflaged against the shades of autumn beauty.

Were we alone or just lonely together?

Alive or just breathing?

My breathing accelerated.

Bleeding or dying?

Sinking or swimming?

Dead or alive?

Fighting or taking flight?

I turned around, looking at the darkening sky. The road was suddenly a long way behind us.

Flight.

My legs were prepared to put as much distance between me and the forest as humanly possible.

'It's fine.' She turned round to look at me. 'I've been this way a million times,' she said, her eyes an animalistic, harlequin green.

I flexed my lungs, inhaling the rancid stench of wilting flowers.

I heard the rush of a river.

If you get lost, follow the water, I reminded myself.

Stupidly, I did not listen.

Shaking off the chill that crawled up my spine, I took a few steps, catching up to her, forsaking the light for someone else's comfort.

4:34 PM

'Do you have a nickname?' Galatea asked, ghostly irises boring into mine.

'No, not really.'

'Do you want one?'

'Haven't thought about it. Do you have one?'

'No, but I've thought about it. I've been called a lot of things, though, like Dirtbag, Stumpy, Dozy, Wrecking Ball, Gingernut, Maurice (don't ask), Valentina, Kentucky Fried Chicken, Box Child and Henny,' she said, ticking them off on her fingertips.

'Kentucky Fried Chicken?'

'Yes.'

I giggled accidentally.

She looked at me expectantly. 'Samm—'

'Don't call me Sammy.'

'Okay... Samson.'

A bird chirped, sounding like an exclamation of happiness. I looked for the bird in the mess of bony tree branches and raked-up piles of leaves.

It was a very big thicket.

The afternoon drifted into eventide, and goosebumps raised the dark hairs on my arms.

Galatea turned to me, her eyes—so pale they could have cataracts—reflecting the near non-existent light.

4:59 PM

The only things twixt us were a slice of air, half a metre and her breath, pooling in white clouds due to the cold. She offered me her hand. I took it, wrapping my cold fingers around her hot flesh. Obviously, my blazer was not enough to help me fight the brunt of the late October weather.

We walked a bit farther with no sign of the other side of the thicket.

Her shiny eyes flitted about, pupils almost lost in the pearlescent whiteness. They were like a cat's eyes, green and iridescent.

'Do you think we're close?' I asked as the weak traces of light started to dwindle.

My accomplice audibly sniffled. 'God, I don't know!' she sobbed.

'So, we're lost?' I inquired, scoffing. I let go of her hand, embarrassed I had even been holding it in the first place.

'Duh!' she snapped.

'I knew it! I knew I should have left when I could still see the road,' I said, running a hand through my hair, mussing it. 'Do you have a torch?'

'Not a very good one, though.' She wiped her eyes, cleaning away the tears that shone like silver skylines on her face.

Galatea reached into her blazer pocket and pulled out a small keyring torch. She clicked it lightly, and a damp-looking beam of light burst from the spherical LED.

'Why would you lead us here if you didn't know where we were going?' I shouted at her, louder than I'd intended.

'Just stop! I made a mistake, okay?' Tears continued to dribble down her face, gleaming and metallic. As the teardrops fell, they sizzled on the dry leaves like the remnants of a fire. She wiped her eyes with her jumper sleeve, and the sizzling noise returned.

'God, it burns.'

'What do you mean, it burns?' She showed me her sleeve and how it was speckled with tiny holes. Through the pinprick holes, I saw that her skin was covered in red welts.

'Okay, so you've got a rash. We're lost, and it's your fault. Don't try to change the subject.'

She pricked, tilting her head visibly in a feline manner. 'Just stop for a second,' she commanded, turning off the torch. 'There's something here.'

We crouched behind a particularly thick oak tree, still moving as one.

'Why'd you turn off the torch? Even if there is something, just because we can't see it doesn't mean it can't see us,' I whispered angrily.

I felt her body move forward in the in complete blackness. A branch cracked, but it was beneath neither my feet nor hers. Maybe she was right. Maybe there was something out there.

'Can't you see them?' Galatea murmured. Her eyes practically glowed within their sockets.

I heard things everywhere: heavy steps, clumsy feet, hopping birds and…something I had never heard before. Nevertheless, it chilled me down to the bone.

It was the sound of a gun being cocked.

'I can't see them anymore,' she said, not hearing the things I could, I surmised.

I tried to tell her to shut up, but the words wouldn't come.

She began to stand up, not caring about being heard. 'I guess it's okay.' Something faintly pink was stuck in her arm. She looked up at me, and the silver had faded from her eyes, leaving her with a haunted look.

'Crap, it's tranquil—' and she fell into my arms, limp in twenty seconds or less.

We *were* on a farmer's land—perhaps that's why we had been targeted.

I stood completely still, trying to delay what was coming, but they had me cornered.

'Damn kids,' said the shooter.

I barely had the time to process the situation before I was under fire.

The last things I saw were the pink fletching from an oncoming dart and the sky, dark grey s—

A DOG WITH NO BITE

5

My eyes opened, though I couldn't remember going to bed.

Where is she?

Who?

HER.

Oh.

It was like Samantha all over again.

Losing somebody.

Letting them slip through my fingers.

She was right there—

—and I let her go.

It wasn't our fault—

—where did she go?

Where did *I* go?

Where *am* I?

I opened my eyes properly.

My body suddenly woke up, and I felt everything everywhere.

Blood rushed to my knuckles, as they rubbed raw on the jagged floor.

I was moving…being dragged…

Being dragged?

Yeah, that was it: being dragged.

Thoughts slipped out of my head, doing loops and twirls and splattering themselves on the walls of my skull.

My hands were numb and immobile.

The hallway was dark. The polished, indigo tiles had been scratched by inhuman claws.

Something was dragging me with cold, wet fingers.

I tried to scream but found my neck bound with a metal cuff. It was so *tight*.

I swallowed heavily, gulping down the saliva in my throat.

The fingers pulled roughly at my cuff, making me feel like a dog.

I twisted my neck as much as possible, trying to catch a glimpse of my captor.

Their face was just out of sight, like fold-worn Polaroid people, lost forever in a branching white crease.

The corridor journey lasted for an eternity and then some.

Was this an abduction?

Was this what it meant to be kidnapped?

Just let me die.

I was yanked abruptly to my feet by the blurry person in a three-piece made of colours that left my mind as soon as they left my line of sight. Colours like feldgrau[2] and glaucous[3] blended together. Colours full of anemoia and the longing for a home that wasn't mine.

Home.

Had they even noticed my absence?

My arms were still dead, but my legs were beginning to respond.

In front of me were grand, wooden, double doors like those on Shakespeare's Globe.

---

[2] German grey.
[3] Powdery blue.

The person behind me shoved my noodle-like body through the doors. Much to my surprise, it didn't hurt.

The inside of the room was pitch black, but it was a different type of black than the forest. The forest had been an open, ebony black, but the room was a closed, boxed-up kind of sable.

Through the thin, fuzzy darkness, the room appeared to be laid out like a cinema, with rows and rows of carpet-like seats upholstered with snazzy-looking, eighties-era covers.

I was shoved down the aisle until I reached the top of the steps, where I was forced into the nearest seat and held down by invisible hands as the faceless three-piece cuffed my hands to the chair.

Only, they weren't cuffs. They were something much thicker and much heavier, like arm gauntlets welded to the chair.

The person in iridescent clothing unlocked my neck cuff, pulling away the chain the instant it opened. The sound of footsteps receded. The captors had gone.

I filled my lungs, preparing to scream my head off.

'Don't,' warned a voice from my right.

'Don't what?' I asked, alarmed by the sudden noise.

'Scream. No doubt your attempt will be fruitless,' replied the voice. She spoke with a thick dose of something foreign and Eastern European, concealed by a mish-mash of posh British dialects. She couldn't have been much older than me.

She coughed, a sickly, rattling sound.

'What's happening? Where are we?' My heart rate accelerated.

'I don't know.'

I didn't care about her answer, I was just glad I wasn't alone. A glimmer of hope rose in my throat. Maybe they'd seen Galatea.

'Have you seen somebody with...with long gingerish hair...ringlets... a hooked nose, and really light green eyes anywhere?' I pleaded as if begging for her life with the Moirai. My heartstrings swelled with longing.

Please, please, please!

'I haven't seen anyone but carbon copies of the one who cut your chain and the outlines of the people on this side of the room. Hate to burst your bubble, but they're probably not here,' she explained, genuinely apologetic.

YOU'RE SO USELESS! You couldn't even save her, and she was right there, in your arms.

I gulped down my disappointment.

'The others—you can see?'

'Of course, there are others. Don't be a solipsist,[4]' she scoffed. 'You just have to be patient. Your eyes will adjust in no time.'

'I didn't know what that meant but I didn't want to ask because I thought it might sound stupid.'

The person turned, physically turned, to face me. 'I'm Brynhild. I assume that was going to be your next question.'

'Samson.'

I don't think she heard me.

---

[4] Solipsism: The idea that only oneself is sure to exist; being selfish or self-centred.

'If not, I don't mean to sound arrogant,' Brynhild muttered, not quite to me and not quite to herself. 'How to say? How to speak?'

I wasn't inclined to respond, too busy retrieving my heart from the pit of my stomach.

The black fog in front of my eyes cleared, and I was finally able to see, not well, but at least I could see.

Her hair was a wintry blonde, like porcelain against the muddy ivory of her skin, bound together in messy pigtails that curled and writhed unnaturally when they reached their end at her abdomen. Brynhild peered at me with naked, brown, doe eyes speckled with shades of cardinal red and sadness. Their dullness was made indistinct behind her foggy, circular-framed glasses.

I looked down at my body. I was still in my school uniform, albeit a bit dirtier than I remembered— more bloodstained and ripped.

She was in hers too. It was pristine, untarnished and perfect, comprised of a vintage-blue shirt (tucked in, of course), with a deep indigo, argyle-patterned tie wrapped below the doily-like collar. Her skirt rested at the lower thigh in a pleated mess of black and white gingham.

I checked her nails. They were long and jagged, almost glossy, with half-bitten, thistle-coloured nail polish that pooled at the cuticles. I knew she looked posh—no public school would have allowed nail polish.

'I—' Brynhild began. She was cut off by dappled scene lights that burst to life at the front of the room.

As I had suspected, there was a stage.

It was like any other stage in the sense that it had curtains, a backdrop and lights to make the 'performance' visible.

The curtains rippled, twitched, and finally rose.

I was unsurprised to see a blurry person approach the edge of the stage, holding a microphone. I guess I half-expected a musical ensemble to burst out of the wings and serenade the smear of grey. Obviously, that did not happen.

'Hello, children. Do not be afraid,' he began in a voice sounding like a radio on the fritz. The sound waves coming from his mouth morphed the air, moulding it to accept his nimble form.

'Madame H will be with you shortly. Now, I must ask you to behave,' he hissed.

'What is this all about, do you think?' Brynhild whispered, feeling silenced by the space around us.

I didn't reply.

A second person walked out onto the raised platform, holding some type of outdated microphone. This one wasn't grey or blurry. She was as vibrant and human as could be. Her hair was so deeply black that it took on a bluish tinge, complementing her solely maroon attire. She smiled with teeth so big and white they were almost equine. The superficial show of happiness beamed light onto the rows nearest the front, which were, as Brynhild had mentioned, full of other people.

Schoolchildren like us.

'I know you have already been welcomed, so I shan't do it again. You've been invited here to participate in a series of tests. Some will be written papers, others tests of physical abilities. Either way, they are a part of our program to, in short, make you the best version of yourselves you can be.'

She waited for even a single chuckle, but no one made a sound.

Madame H cleared her throat. 'Your living arrangements have been made. If you have any concerns, problems or questions, my office is open twenty-four-seven, or you can talk to anyone on the Osprey Team.'

The lights changed direction, shining on some people above us in the gods' area. They were all wearing hooked masks that seemed to be made of something like silver gilt, reflecting the light into my eyes, making their cranberry-red cloaks appear ultramarine. 'Or the *Griseo Promptu*, who brought you to your seats,' she finished and strutted sulkily off the stage.

What the heck was this place? What on earth had I done to deserve being abducted and taken to this awful place? They say your past catches up with you, but it had only been a year. I've had dreams of hell before but none like this.

I didn't want to die here.

It's a silly thought but it was the only thought on my mind. I never thought I'd be the type to be scared of death, but I didn't deserve this. I could see it: my gravestone or my urn. Fourteen meaningless years of a dreary grey life and then a trip to the abattoir.

I didn't want to die here.

Our handcuffs simultaneously unlocked, leaving me with aching hands and raw wrists. Most, if not all, of us leapt up from our seats. Some of them even tried to make a dash for the door.

'Shall we exit?' Brynhild asked me, brushing a stray strand of hair behind her ear.

I didn't reply. I just walked towards the door, going to the back of the queue that was forming.

Brynhild followed suit.

I peered over the heads of the writhing crowd, searching for my lost friend's copper hair. I looked for pieces of her, anything from my reality that would tell me she was still alive, still there. I would settle for anything: the ghostly celadon glint of her eyes, the bruises on her face, even the freckles on her skin.

Something—anything—familiar.

The queue filtered out into the hallway, and I realised we were being pushed out by the *Griseo Promptu*. Some were up ahead, shepherding us into a relatively small atrium with a curved stained glass ceiling, depicting the Holy Eucharist, chalice and all. The window had hundreds if not thousands of intricate pieces carefully carved into various geometric shapes, coloured green, red, yellow, blue and the purest of whites. Holding it onto the roof of the small gathering place was a gold vermeil frame decorated with Sweet Williams and poppies made out of ruby and garnet. At the edge of the room was a dual staircase, leading somewhere that was shrouded from view.

In the midst of all the noise, one of the blurry people stood up, supported by two of their colleagues. All three of them read off the names and rooms, barely giving the girls enough time to think.

'Alcoy, Annabel,' they read from a clipboard, 'floor one, room one,' they said, pointing to the winding stairs. The crowd was disturbed as Annabel (I assume) pushed forward to stand on the stairs.

'Beauregard, Matilda... floor one, room one.'

'Butch, Isabella... floor two, room one.'

'Carter, Veronica... floor one, room four.'

'Cavanaugh, Talia... floor one, room one.'

Talia, the most recent to be called, wandered to the right staircase instead of the one on the left like everyone else; the deviation was not missed.

The taller of the three grey workers clicked their fingers and pointed angrily to the left.

Talia shuddered and ran to where she was supposed to be.

'Davis, Richard... floor one, room four.'

The person holding the clipboard pointed sharply to the left.

'Evans, Harvey... floor two, room one.'

To be honest, I kind of zoned out until they reached Brynhild, sending her to floor one, room three.

I wouldn't be seeing her again.

From there on, it was just a sea of names I didn't recognise.

A few minutes after Brynhild had been called, I heard a name I definitely knew: 'Machezelli, Sylvia...floor two, room four.'

Where did I know that name from? It was faded and worn and it bounced around on my tongue, but why? I couldn't, for the life of me, match a face to the name. Sylvia, whoever she was, was nothing more than the feeling of summer and decaying happiness.

I had little time to contemplate it because they then read out a name that rang clear as day in my head: 'Owens, Galatea...floor one, room three.'

Floor one, room three.

'Elliot, Timothy... floor two, room four.'

'Frond-Smith, Walter...floor one, room two.'

'Geller, Ash...floor two, room four.'

'Hyûga, Pygmalion...floor one, room three.'

'Ostrovsky, Samson...floor one, room three.'

I heard my name and made my way to the front as politely as possible.

Floor one, room three.

I couldn't even look at her. I had to wait till we were upstairs.

'Perez, Aphrodite...floor one, room three.' Nine more names were read. Soon, there were forty or so of us standing around the staircase. Upon seeing the congregation, the person with the clipboard pointed to the right. 'If you are bound for floor one, use the right stairs.'

The crowd immediately cleared.

'Be off,' the short one commanded with a flick of their tubby wrist, and the groups ascended the stairs almost silently.

I ran.

6

ROOM 3
It read on the plaque above the door.

Room three.

This was real. We were in the middle of nowhere, having been whisked away by people in masks, and there was nothing we could do to save ourselves.

I wrapped my fingers around the engraved doorknob and pulled, forcing my muscle tissues to stretch to their limit. It opened with a long, grating *SCREECH,* permitting me entry.

I walked in, feeling my shoes track mud on the softwood floor, gazed around the room, and I felt guilty for the mess.

The ceiling was quite high (about twelve feet) and curved, with swirling shades of blue and white forming something like *L'Apothéose d'Hercule.*[5] Rugs peppered the floor everywhere, from outside the bathrooms to beneath the long, clear windows, under the downstairs sofa, and in front of the barred fireplace.

Inside the relatively large room, there was a small staircase with a wide, amethyst-purple, carpeted landing.

The room was staged with a miscellany of furniture: a sticky-looking, white, houndstooth loveseat overshadowed by a stick-like black lamp; two opaque glass, glossy coffee tables; a cushy, sage green armchair; a pair of stools covered with Skobeloff satin and a black, velvet settee.

---

[5] The Apotheosis of Hercules.

Hanging from the centre of the separate, lower ceiling were hand-blown glass light bulbs, lying dead with shells of amber and violet.

In the main room, beneath the arch of the upstairs space, were two twin-sized Murphy beds, held above the ground by sleek, iridescent chains.

The beds were not made, but the duvets were tucked under the mattresses, and the pillows were at the heads of the beds. The empty bed space had nooks with necessities inside, like toothbrushes, sponges, shower gels and sprays.

Above the bed closest to the window was a rather big vent that rattled wetly, as if it were breathing hot air into the room.

The others arrived behind me, and I pointed at them to take off their shoes, like me.

There were two strangers. Towering over me by at least a few inches was a boy with greasy, black hair, dull, curled and drooping—probably unintentionally—over his forehead. His lips were scaly but not dry or damaged, in the same way a snake looks sleek and wet whilst in the desert. His jawline was soft but clenched, defining his faint cheekbones. He was faintly olive-skinned but so sickly that, though he looked green, it complemented his deep umber monolid eyes that tracked my every move.

'What are you looking at?' he asked me, clenching his jaw. He had a muted Geordie accent that only made him seem more threatening.

I averted my gaze.

It seemed as if Galatea and Brynhild hadn't arrived yet.

Behind him was a girl (I think) with droopy shoulders and half-closed eyes, crisscrossing red veins reaching for her pupils. Her skin was brown but unhealthy-looking, stretched thinly over the delicate canvas of her face. The girl's French bob was dyed web browser blue on the tips of her pecan-brown hair, making it look sandy, fake and damaged.

I gave her a half-hearted smile. She put her middle finger up at me and mouthed something that looked like 'Pervert.'

I was about to turn and run before the very person I'd been waiting for walked through the doorway.

'Found the friend,' Brynhild said, forcing the friend through the doorway.

In strode Galatea confidently…until she saw me and her demeanour changed to less tense, bolder.

'And now, privacy for these two,' they almost sang, probably trying to make the best of a bad situation. As instructed, Pygmalion (the tall one) and Aphrodite (the rude one) followed Brynhild upstairs after inviting us to have a private conversation.

I checked behind me. They weren't watching.

'How do I—' The words fell dead on my tongue. How could I apologise if there was nothing left to say?

She stood just a few inches away, unsure how to react. I was, too—unsure, I mean—so we trembled together, the six inches between us feeling shockingly close to six feet.

My lungs felt far too big for my ribcage, and my eyes stung but not with the unadulterated loathing they had earlier. Now it was more like relief, happiness.

I coughed down the bitterness in my throat. Before I knew it, her arms were wrapped tightly around me, and she wept into my chest. I squeezed her back, resting my head on hers. The smell of her skin wafted up into my nostrils. Galatea smelled fresh and earthy, like the roots of a weed or the petals of a rose. At the same time, it was a sort of nutty chamomile scent, like evaporated moisture with a sweet atmosphere.

I bit my lip and let the tears flow with no need to look for an excuse.

'Sorry,' she mumbled, still holding my school jumper close to her face.

'Don't say that. You have nothing to be sorry for,' I reassured her, even though it was only partially true.

'It's okay. You don't need to infantilise me. I know it was my fault.'

'No…no.'

I let go, keeping my hand on her shoulder.

'I got us shot!'

'I was too loud.'

'You don't understand,' she sobbed, 'I could see him, and I…I…I *know* he wouldn't have shot us if we'd run, but I stood there like an IDIOT, deer in headlights style, and waited. Waited for him to come for us. Almost as if I wanted it—like…like—'

She cut off abruptly, shivering and gasping. Her nose was red like the rims of her eyes, and I could see how she struggled, coughing and spluttering to get the words out of her mouth.

I recoiled out of instinct and hoped she didn't notice.

'L-like I…I wanted him t-to kill us. And…I…' Galatea leaned against the wall and slid down onto the shiny, plywood floor. Her hair knotted and tangled, getting stuck to the textured wallpaper. She buried her head in her hands.

'She'll be so worried,' she mumbled, probably talking about her foster mum.

'Good. If she's out looking, we're more likely to be found,' I said, abnormally sanguine.

'Don't you think your parents'll be worried, too?'

'No.'

'Why not?'

I reached for my elbow and ran my finger over the long, knobbly scab along the bone. 'They don't like me too much.' I scratched at it, searching for the courage to peel.

'Is it because of Samantha?' At that, Galatea looked up at me.

My fingernails made a sharp movement, and I broke the hardened skin, coating my fingernails in wet, mushy scab tissue and dried pus. Even the mere mention of her name turned the world on its head. The space behind my eyes boiled again, and my teeth chattered even though I wasn't cold in the slightest.

It felt as if she'd impaled me with something blunt and heavy. I thought I was getting better at living with my sister's absence, but that was none of her *damn* business.

'We won't open Pandora's box today,' I told her, not meeting her eyes, standing there with my fingers begored and covered in cold, cold blood.

It took everything in me not to scream at her.

When I had made it clear to Galatea that I didn't want to talk about my problems with her, we rejoined the group upstairs.

'Nice room,' she remarked, looking around.

'Mm-hm.'

Trekking up the stairs proved a lot more complicated than expected, requiring me to cling to the banister for much-needed support. I wobbled, put off balance by the differences between the steps—whoever had fitted the stairs had not been the least bit professional.

Trying to make my breathing sound natural, I stumbled onto the landing, feeling the virtually untouched carpet through my stiff, sweaty school socks.

'Glad you are back. Have you met either of these two?' Brynhild asked. I looked at the other two strangers. They sat cross-legged on the loveseat. Aphrodite was slouched impolitely on the back of the same chair as Brynhild, and Pygmalion scooted towards one corner of the velvet sofa, inviting us to sit. We took the invitation, and Galatea nodded at him to say thank you.

I opened my mouth to begin talking *at* Aphrodite but closed it when I received her hard, icy stare.

'That's a no?' Brynhild said.

'Yes, it is,' I said.

Brynhild looked at Aphrodite expectantly.

'Aphrodite Perez, sixteen years old, Air Cadet,' she said monotonously.

He nodded, looking less pale and anxious. 'My name is Pygmalion Hyûga. I am an only child, fifteen years old, and I have two cats, Moxie and Blossom (or Bloss).' He smiled. 'Nice to meet you.' Pygmalion raised his hand in a motionless wave to substitute for a handshake or anything like that.

I smiled back, forgetting that Galatea was next to me.

Brynhild cleared their throat and made the jazziest of hands. 'You *all* know me, but I'm Brynhild Durchdenwald, youngest (and favourite) of six, fourteen years old, choir kid, form captain, gymnast, bilinguist and hockey captain.' She giggled. 'Those are just a few of my achievements.'

Talk about an over-achiever!

'No one asked.' Aphrodite rolled her eyes and jumped off of the sofa.

'Moody.' Brynhild sighed. 'So, what about you two?' she pointed at Galatea and me.

'Enough of the small talk!' I said, annoyed. 'Will someone tell us what is going on?'

'He's right," Aphrodite remarked. She looked at Pygmalion, 'We have to tell them.'

Pygmalion sighed and nodded. I heard the blood rushing in my ears. What could possibly explain all that'd happened and what was still to come?

'"I'll try and explain this briefly. This is an experiment that will play on the strongest of your human emotions.

For example, mine is spite, Pygmalion's is anger and yours, Brynhild, judging from that short excerpt, is inferiority.

'You two,' she turned to Galatea and me, 'you'll know what yours is. Everyone knows deep down: we're all aware of our flaws. Whether or not we choose to show them is up to the individual.'

Nothing she said made any sense, but I knew what mine was nonetheless. I meant to stand up and shout in confusion, but I couldn't move an inch. I couldn't even blink. I just stared, fixated on Aphrodite, soaking up her words.

'That's bull.'

I looked to my right, and sure enough, Galatea was doing what I couldn't. She'd crossed her arms, cocked her head and refused to accept the situation.

Pygmalion rose from his seat and stepped out to stand beside Aphrodite.

'It's not. You have to understand,' he looked me dead in the eyes, 'whether or not you agree with their methods, whether or not you think the experiment is fruitless, you have to carry on. After this conversation, you *will* continue as if you know nothing. I guarantee everyone else will act the same.'

'How do you know all this? Why am I supposed to trust you?' Galatea's voice blended into the background. I glanced at Brynhild. Her eyes had gone dark, and she seemed just as shocked as I was, except she seemed as though she was retreating into herself, looking for something.

'We don't have all the answers,' Aphrodite said, stepping in, stoic and monotonous. 'Even if we did, you wouldn't get it. All you have to know is that your strongest emotions are your weaknesses.'

'The aim of the experiment is to erase them. You've been picked because you were in the wrong place at the wrong time— or rather, the right place, right time. They look for emotion. They feed on it.

'You're here because they *found* you. We've been handpicked. We're going to be inhuman,' he continued.

As soon as he said 'erase', I perked up. If this experiment could get rid of the gnawing pain in my chest, if I could lift the weight I'd been forced to bear, it was *worth* it. I didn't want to carry around guilt, to have it trail after me like a stray dog. I didn't care about being inhuman. I just wanted to have at least one good night's sleep. I wanted one night that I didn't think about her. These experiments, they'd only hurt for a moment. They'd only be uncomfortable for a second. The relief from my guilt would last a lifetime.

It was then I decided I'd do it. I'd reach out and grab the opportunity with both hands. It might burn my palms, it might send electricity through my veins like lightning rods, but it would only be for a second in the grand scheme of things.

It would only hurt for a second.

'Simply put,' Aphrodite sighed, 'war is coming if you want it. War is coming if you don't. And whether or not you accept the call to arms is not up to you.'

Galatea furrowed her eyebrows. 'I don't want this.'

'No one does.'

I mustered up the strength to stand. 'I don't want it; I need it,' I said, with the most certainty I'd ever felt in my life. My voice had not trembled. and it had not cracked.

It would only hurt for a second.

7

The uncomfortable silence hung in the air like a bad smell until Brynhild awoke from her stupor and started rambling on about beds. It hadn't properly dawned on me that we were going to have to sleep there. Even Aphrodite and Pygmalion looked confused.

After a whole lot of searching, we found three more beds. They were awkward features, protruding from beneath the downstairs windows, with feathery mattresses and retractable frames. Subsequently, I was nominated to go find bedsheets, which I did without hesitation—the people in my room weren't the best.

I stepped out into the cold, church-like hallway, searching for any indication that sheets had been left out for us. Instead, I found three other doors next to ours.

Curiosity got the better of me, and I knocked on the door labelled ROOM 4, which was to the right of our door.

It was answered almost immediately by a boy with a neeky fringe and gold-rimmed glasses. Even before he'd said a word, I tried to guess what his emotion was. I wondered if I wore mine on my sleeve. I wondered if the others knew.

"Ello," he said in a tone that implied an unsaid 'What do you want?'

'Do you know where the bedsheets are?'

'Right down the 'all, I fink,' he said.

'Thanks,' I nodded, striding over to door number one. They weren't there, so I knocked.

'It's open.'

I knocked again, even though I'd been told it was open.

'Dammit! It is **OPEN**. Come **IN**!' the person shouted, emphasising the last words of each sentence.

Of course, I entered. The room was a tiny bit different than ours. For instance, the colour scheme was red, blue and yellow instead of purple and green. A girl with blue-tinted passion twists and a nose ring was tying up her shoelaces by the door.

'Do you know where the bedsheets are?'

'They're upstairs, outside of room one,' she told me, completely contradicting the blond boy.

Feeling betrayed, I went upstairs and got the sheets, avoiding saying anything to anyone on the way back.

When I returned, I dressed my allocated sleeping area (the Murphy bed closest to the window) with the lime green sheets, purposefully avoiding Galatea and any questions she might want to ask me. I checked my watch: 24:64 PM.

I looked at it again. Clear as day, that was what the numbers said: 24:64 PM.

'That can't be right.'

I took off the watch, threw it behind the bed and stared out of the window.

The evening sky was peppered with cyclamen-coloured clouds. Ribbons of divine gold, left by the evanescent sun, danced elegantly in the sky. The Alice-blue sky faded slightly into a mild mauve. It looked to be sometime around four-thirty to five, the time when the gentleness of light begins to fade.

Brynhild collapsed onto the bed beside me. I sat gingerly on my covers, careful not ruin all of my hard work.

'I miss Mutter,' she said, muffled by the pillow, 'and I bet Daddy misses me.'

'I—'

'*Hör auf zu reden!* I'm not done.'

'What?'

'Do not talk... Stop.

'So anyway, my problems...' She went on and ON about things I didn't care about, but I still listened politely and gave input at the correct intervals. Something about all of her friends being two-faced or something like that. Something only empty-headed girls had the privilege to worry about.

'You know what, Hild? I'm just gonna…take a quick nap, and I'll be with you fully after that,' I said, taking off my blazer.

'Oh,' she mumbled, crestfallen. 'You know, I think they have a closet in the nook.' She pointed to the weird handle-like thing on the back wall of the space the Murphy beds tucked into.

I crawled up to the top of my bed, grabbed the handle and yanked as hard as I could. The crusty little compartment burst open.

As Brynhild said, there were various clothing items hung up and tucked away in the closet. The outfits were all monochrome, either green, purple or yellow, arranged in their own sad, lonely rainbow. I snatched a tee shirt and knee-length shorts and walked off to the bathroom to get changed before dropping like a dead weight onto my bed.

8

My eyes snapped open of their own accord. A feeling of hopelessness washed over my body. I just stared at the ceiling, the same ceiling I was under a whole day ago. In the same bed, it seemed, with the same broken springs, hardened glue and sweet wrappers hidden in the duvet. They would've been gone if anyone had bothered to tidy them up. Mum sure wasn't fit to do it, and I had this deal with the maid that she cleaned where and when she wanted to, and I stayed out of her way.

I looked over, searching for my bookcases on the other side of the room, but I didn't see them. Nor did I see my lamp. Come to think of it, the room was unusually dark, as I always slept with the lights on.

I sat up, frantically observing the things around me. I wasn't alone.

On the adjacent bed was Brynhild, identified by her practically luminescent blonde hair trickling onto the floor.

If she was with me—

Then I'm not—

I was still there.

I didn't go home, and this wasn't my bed. It was...it was... it was the same one I'd slept in last night.

Crap.

The truth became clear to me when I referred to my true crime knowledge: I was never going home.

By now, maybe Mum would miss me. Maybe she'd realised something was wrong, that she'd taken me for granted when her favourite little 'Sapphire' sunk like the Titanic.

I remember when I'd set the whole thing in motion, when she'd begun to plan it: the 26th of June, 2003.

It was a year-long commitment to a suicide that she didn't even want to effectuate. She just wanted to perform and be the star of the show again. Her death truly wasn't a scream or a plea to an unloving, uncaring world. It was, if stripped down to its bare bones, her having something to prove, that everything was wrong with our family, that a tiny ripple would be enough to distort the perfect mirror image.

Smart.

It'd been a Monday, a sunny one that replaced the gloominess of the previous year's summer sunsets. Periodical cicadas emerged for the first time in my life, leaving their golden shells all around the garden.

We sat down for something like a latchkey-kid dinner (a box of partially defrosted prawns for me and a cup of pot noodles for my sister), eating in silence as usual.

'So, are we going to talk about him?' Samantha said, moving her chopsticks around in her cup, breaking the silence.

'D-do you w-want to?' I said, coughing, nearly choking.

'Yes, Samson, I do. I kind of brought him up so we *would* talk about him.' She was cocky now, slurping meanly.

'Well, there's really nothing to say. His name was Axel Hepworth, and we had two lessons together: science and textiles. I stabbed him with a pen once because he wouldn't shut up, and he liked me. A lot, I mean. He would laugh at my jokes and write me cute messages.' I shrugged and pushed away the empty plastic container.

'Saying what?'

I smiled dreamily for a brief second before snapping back. 'That he loved me.' I know she saw it.

'He said he LOVED you? He didn't even want ME. Why on EARTH would he want somebody like you?' she spat, suddenly bitter about my missing friend and her recently-stoked flame of infatuation. 'But he didn't want you for long,' she murmured, fully intending for me to hear.

'Have you ever even considered the fact that I'm a *different* person than you? You're not better than me. In fact, we aren't even comparable,' I flared up, defending myself and the sliver of hope that told me Axel would come back to us.

'It's like comparing t.A.T.u and Tegan and Sara. Both of them are great, but one of them is less successful, talented and valued.'

'So I'm t.A.T.u?'

'No, 'cause Axel's into t.A.T.u.!'

I stood up.

'Oh, my God. For Chrissake—he's *missing!* And you can't even... you can't...' My words couldn't decide which of them should go first. I felt the tears coming, but I pulled them back, continuing with a steadily rising volume and shaky voice. 'I'm done. You're so inconsistent, not just here but everywhere. You want to be so subversive, but you follow a movement.' I threw up my hands in defeat. 'You think you're rebelling, that you're *different,* but all you're doing is becoming a *different* branch of basic. And all for a boy you'll forget in a few years,' I caught my breath and took another blow at her.

I should've been used to Samantha being so insensitive by now.

'He might not come back, you know. He's done this before, but you didn't know, did you? Because people don't exist until they come into your own little world, where the earth bloody revolves around you! They don't have lives, minds or agendas until you take an interest or somebody else gets there first. That's what it was, wasn't it? You saw him sitting with me behind the bike shed, and you thought, *Oh, how do I ruin my brother's life this time? Maybe I could flirt with his "friend",* but you saw us, didn't you?

'And you knew—God, you knew so well—that I would drag myself over the third rail to keep what he and I had, but you went and ruined it with your gangly friends and their threats. You always want what you can't have and you couldn't have him! You *chased* him away just to move on to some other boy you think wants you around. You as good as *killed* him.'

'It's not my fault,' my sister began, trying to blame something she had both thought out and executed on the boy who had run from one type of hell to another.

'Oh, yeah? 'Cause nothing ever is, is it?'

I stormed upstairs to cry, I think.

She shouted things after me about how she was sorry and that she would do anything for me not to tell Mum and Dad. As if I could.

I screamed down at her, torn in half by the realisation that the one person who had made an effort to even seem as if he valued me was gone.

After a while, she got bored of the comforting and began plotting her final endeavour (because she knew I'd never let it go), starting with the date I saw written in her notebook: 24/10/2004.

And she sure stuck to schedule.

9

I fell asleep to tortured thoughts of Axel: broken, bloody, alive, asleep and…dead.

It was something I'd imagined millions of times, his unblemished, lily-white skin torn and red with stitches along his body, purulent, jaundiced scar tissue leaking serous fluid from his neck.

It was weird thinking about him when I had previously tried to forget his existence altogether. Now that I'm older, I think it might have just been pheromones or something explained through science. That doesn't mean I didn't love him—I was ready to fight if it meant keeping the one good thing I had to myself. I was prepared to stomach anything for him, for somebody who made me feel wanted and loved, for somebody who needed me, kept me from snapping completely in two and giving into my tendency to rip into everything good and sacred.

He was so nice, with a smile radiant enough to light up an entire town during a power outage. And his voice… it was so…beautiful as if his words alone could improve my day.

I remembered him as the sun filtered through my eyelashes, appearing fig purple in the morning light. I hoped that wherever he was, he was being treated well, but I know that loving a person from too far away to drive isn't the same as loving him in person.

Maybe I just liked the idea of him.

Despite this, I covered my face with crossed arms as my heart bled for him. It was strange how the place brought him back to me.

I heard footsteps coming toward my bed, sticky, thick and pained, and a pillow suddenly crashed over my head with the force of a storm.

'Wake UP!' came Galatea's angry tone from above.

Great. The very person I'd been trying to avoid wanted to begin the day with a confrontation.

I mumbled something subconsciously.

'One job, that's all I ask. Wake up!' She batted the pillow over my head repeatedly, showing no sign of yielding.

'Hi,' I crackled. The word came out gravelly, as if I'd rubbed cement over my uvula.

'Do you have any idea what time it is?'

'No.'

'Me neither.' She laughed and raised her almost invisible eyebrows.

I rolled out of bed without fear of the cold, hard ground.

I emerged from the bathroom, cleansed and dressed in something I'd pulled from the clothes nook. It wasn't a fashion statement, but it also wasn't offensive to the eyes, so I was not too bothered.

Galatea was already clothed in a yellow paisley shirt-dress, her ribs squeezed to the breaking point by the black belt wrapped around her mid-waist.

Aphrodite was crouched in the corner of the room like a vulture, applying makeup to complete her look. She wore a green turtleneck and a slightly purple skirt. She peered over at Pygmalion while applying her lipstick.

He was in a lilac crew neck and some dark grey cargo pants that fitted him more perfectly than any of mine ever did.

I examined the room. Something felt off. Someone was missing.

As soon as the thought entered my head, Brynhild strode out of the bathroom wearing…something. It looked like a pencil skirt, but flowy and with a slit. It wasn't bad. It was just… something. 'TIME TO CARPE THEM DIEMS!' she shouted, waving around the puffed sleeves of their dress. It was quite pretty, with a William Morris-esque pattern printed on the green, flowy material. Inside the dress was a silky bodice and skirt, enveloped by a translucent chiffon that only went down to just above her knees. Her hair was knotted in a professional-looking bun, but her trademark pigtails still visible. I was beginning to dislike Brynhild very much. I got the sense she was one of those girls who thought she was better than everyone. Somehow, she managed to turn imprisonment into a fashion show.

'Is that my hairband?' I heard Galatea ask.

Brynhild scoffed, making it clear she had stolen her hairband. 'No. 'Course not,' she said.

'What the hell?'

'It's in good hair now, darling.'

Galatea shot her a disapproving look.

Pygmalion smiled at the pair. 'Well, I think you both look lovely.'

Galatea's was better.

Brynhild made a series of half-baked gestures, all seeming to convey the message, 'I told you.'

I was beginning to see her inferiority. She peacocked at the first chance she got.

I tried to cool down the situation before Galatea skinned Brynhild from head to toe (or vice-versa). 'Let's go see where we're supposed to be, and—'

'Where we can get some DAMN food!' Aphrodite said, finishing my sentence for me, rising from her crouching position.

They all seemed to agree with Aphrodite, and they followed me out of the door and down the winding stone staircase. The pressure of being the leader when I had no idea where I was going was terrifying.

'What do you think the experiments will be like?' I asked, directing the question at Aphrodite.

'Hell if I know,' she responded with a tone that sounded like a shrug.

'How did you know enough to explain, then?' Galatea chimed in with a notably more forceful tone.

'The grey ones pulled two from each room aside so that we could explain to the rest of you. I don't know why they couldn't have just mentioned it in the stupid, pretentious assembly instead of making me put in the effort. All I know is that if and when we get out of here, our humanity won't come with us.'

'Why's there going to be a war in the first place? Why do they need us? Why do they need inhuman, children, with no combat training whatsoever?'

'I don't know. I mean, they fully dumped all of these concepts on us and read out our deepest, darkest flaws— I'm sorry I didn't stick around for the Q&A,' she spat.

'Oh, sorry,' Galatea mumbled, and I thought I could hear her shrinking with shame.

The line dispersed. Pygmalion and Brynhild chased the split ends of Aphrodite's moody blue hair as she disappeared around the corner.

'I don't like her,' Galatea stated as soon as they were all out of earshot.

'I don't want to cause rifts in our—'

'Just say you don't like her. It's less effort.'

'Maybe I do like her."

Galatea sighed and ran off to catch up with everyone else.

We arrived at the doors of the main hall, which was the only place we really knew in the expansive building and pushed open the doors. The room was practically filled, indicating it was where we were supposed to be.

Our arrival was extremely loud in the silence of the vast hall. We found two seats and sat down, the subject of everyone's collective gaze.

Madame H had only just reached the microphone. She cleared her throat and said, 'Today, floor one will be engaging in perception, auditory and visual examination. Floor two, however, will participate in blood compatibility, DNA and immune strength testing, respectively. You will swap over in a fortnight, and four weeks from now, you'll be given new examinations to partake in. You will be led to your separate wings by the Osprey. After today, you may be able to navigate the buildings, but if not, go to where you think you're meant to be.' She huffed into the microphone. 'That will be all.' She clapped her hands for the lights to turn on.

They clicked on, beaming unnecessary brightness into my eyes.

'Floor one may rise,' boomed a man in a red cloak and identity-concealing mask.

I did as I was told, joined by the majority of my floor.

The man and several of his cohorts formed a V-formation around us like a flock of migrating birds, and we walked out of the hall at a steady pace, with no disturbances or chatter, just the steady march of twenty pairs of feet.

However unsure I felt, I had to remember how much it hurt. I'd do it for my mum, I'd do it for Axel and I'd do it for her memory. I would become numb, one of the crowd. And I would rest easy.

10

'What are we doing? Why can't we take these tests together?' I inquired, feeling vulnerable. I was practically alone in some sort of empty office cubicle with partitions taller than I was. There was a desk between the Osprey examiner on the other side and me. It was the colour of virgin olive oil and had a mechanical tabletop lamp on the side. We were both sitting down, her on a swivelling office chair and I on a wooden stool.

The Osprey unclipped her merlot-red hood and cast it aside, revealing a fully shaven head. Her eyes were covered by a white masquerade disguise with feathers oriented downwards to give her a hint of distress. Her skin seemed thick and extremely pale, taking on a greenish tinge in the warm, tainted lighting.

She pulled a manilla folder out of the desk. 'Don't worry about any of that,' she said, leaning back in her swinging chair.

I hadn't realised, but my hands were shaking.

'This is just a test of perception and the way you think. We do this because it helps us manage and regulate disordered thinking so it won't interfere with the general process. This is a test of perception. We need to gather information about how you see and recognise the world. It will show us how your mind works, and therefore, helps us deal with disordered thinking and psychological or neurological illnesses. It also helps us assess how well you guys work under pressure. It's nothing to be scared of, I promise.' She chuckled as she removed a thick wad of paper from the folder in question, which I managed to catch a glimpse of before it was discarded. It had three words on it, two in black and the other in red. It also had a date.

Two of the words contained V's, I's, 0's and L's. The top one was in red, reading VI0LASKY. The one below it was VLTRAVI0LET. The third was both illegible and written in red, but the date below it wasn't, as it was printed in deep, defined black: 19/6/91.

I read it as a regular date. I was so used to brushing it aside. It was my birthday. Or Saffy's birthday, as those in my life had dubbed it. It wasn't mine to celebrate, so I hadn't since she died.

'I'm going to show you seven photographs at first, then we'll take a break. After that, we'll listen to some audio, and I'll ask for your interpretation. Everything all right?' asked the Osprey, totally interrupting my train of thought.

I shook my head to indicate that everything was very, very wrong, but she ignored me.

'Okay, time to move on to the audio clips—is that fine?'

I hadn't done anything but look at some abstract photos and spew recycled therapy nonsense. If anything, the change would be welcomed.

She pulled out a sleek, curved Powerbook and placed it—open—on the desk. Also out of the desk came a pair of blocky over-ear headphones. She turned the laptop to face me and handed over the headphones. Upon plugging them in, the laptop switched on and asked for the password to an account labelled 'OCTAVIA ORVILLE'.

I was about to point this out before she fixed it herself, typing in something of a long PIN. 'Call me Janine,' she whispered wistfully.

Janine turned the laptop back around just as an application popped up with a list of seven colour-coded tracks corresponding to their numbers. 'Play 1Red.'

I pressed play. It was like the white noise I'd become accustomed to, but different. The track wasn't just random sounds and feelings. It was a repetitive hammering in my head, the thumping of a bat missing its target, an ache, an itch, something of a yearning for solid ground even though I had it. It'll only hurt for a second.

It was like the child of regret and embarrassment, but bitter, sharp and ever-present.

'What do you think it is?' Janine asked.

My tongue found the word I was looking for. 'It's guilt.'

It'll only hurt for a second.

'Interesting. Is that something you have familiarised yourself with?'

'Yes.'

She jotted something down on her clipboard.

I stopped the track. I couldn't listen to it anymore.

'Play 2Orange.'

My fingers automatically clicked the trackpad. 2Orange was twisted and awkward, like garbled transmissions. It felt like blood oozing out of a septic wound, burning all that surrounded it, like a child knocking the pieces off of a thousand-year-long game of chess with a smile and a feeling of pride, gleefully spoiling the end of a book they'd desecrated. It was disease in the most vulnerable part of the body, and the illness was festering, commandeering the mind and soul.

Janine looked at me expectantly. 'And this?'

'Discord…and sickness.'

'As opposing forces?'

'Quite the opposite.'

She took note of it.

'3Yellow, please.'

This time, the transition was smooth because I'd been expecting it. 3Yellow was more like music, with repetitive chiming elements and deep, ethereal whispering. The whispering was indiscernible and shaky as if its beauty were lost in translation. It had a sense of finality to it, like setting a torch to the past or drowning a memory. Things that you won't regret. Things that are truly for the better.

'What do you—'

'Death, but final.'

'Care to elaborate?'

I took off the headphones, shook my head, and began to stand up.

I wanted to push myself down. I had to remember—I had to realise that I needed this.

Janine pulled out a plastic box filled to the brim with sweets and opened it. 'I had been hoping to get through all seven, but I suppose we'll have to do that on Friday.' She sighed as she handed me some peppermints and put on her hood.

'Good work, Samson.'

This made me freeze like a deer in headlights. How long had it been since anyone had said that to me?

How long will it take for you to disappoint her?

Suddenly, I was struck with the undeniable urge to hug her.

Obviously, I didn't.

I took the peppermints and left the room, letting the double-sided doors swing behind me.

Upon walking into the waiting area, I was hit with the gaze of a dozen pairs of eyes and the brilliantly white lights of the sterile hallway. Brynhild and Galatea were waiting together, with Pygmalion opposite them.

Galatea looked me up and down.

'Jesus Christ, who hurt you?'

I ignored her and looked over to Pygmalion.

'You're up,' I told him. He nodded, and I stormed off.

I heard Brynhild whistle at me, but I didn't turn back. I wasn't a dog to be summoned with a whistle and put on a leash. At least, not hers, anyway.

We fling up flowers and laugh; we laugh across the wine;
With wine, we dull our souls and careful strains of art;
Our cups are polished skulls round, which the roses twine:
None dares to look at Death, who leers and lurks apart.

- The Carthusians by Ernest Dowson.

It was a stanza that had been out of reach for weeks. It felt austere, devoid of flavour, like blocks of clear wax sliding from my mouth, hard, vapid and cold.

I put my hand on the mirror, watching the glass fog up above my flesh. The frosted glass windows framed the sheer darkness outside, killing the illusion of sunset. Nights like these were always hard. My eyes itched, and the images they'd burned into my mind flashed through me at night, flying like electricity across my nervous system.

This was more than a second. Three days had felt like a lifetime and we weren't nearly done. My resolve had dwindled and evaporated, down to the very last drop. I was ready to give up.

'You always were so…***weak.***'

I felt a finger on my shoulder, creating ripples in my t-shirt.

You're not real.

I turned around—

and stared at the demon who'd stolen her face

—but she wasn't there.

I wiped the mirror and turned off the tap. It stopped dripping into the almost overflowing bathtub.

'Don't ignore me,' it said.

'Why not?'

SHE'S NOT THERE!

I looked back into the mirror—

She's dead.

—and very nearly screamed.

A calloused beige hand covered my mouth. It smelled of salt and decay.

Samantha laughed maniacally, trembling as the air puffed out of her lungs. In the mirror, I saw the upward tilt of her eyes, lids puffy and red as if she'd been stung by a swarm of bees. 'I could never leave you.'

'But you're **dead**.'

Samantha tilted her head. 'And whose fault is that?'

'Yours, Saffy. I did what you told me.'

'Oh, no, no, no, Sammy, dear. If you didn't deeply want me gone, you wouldn't have taken that step. You wouldn't have pushed me that hard, and you might've even pulled me back from the edge, but you didn't.'

'I miss you. I wish I'd been better.'

'No, you don't. If you did, you'd get help so we could stop meeting so unconventionally. I mean, if you wanted to be healthy, you'd let go and tell someone, but you **can't,** can you? You're so afraid—*oh, so afraid*—that they'll all stare at you with hatred and think, "There's the one who killed his sister. It must've been like murdering his doppelgänger. Who on EARTH would do such a thing to a girl so delicate and beloved? He must be **twisted**!" And who would, except you?' She grinned and laughed her jackal's laugh, licking her teeth with her slimy purple tongue.

'I do. I w-want to—'

'You've had SO many chances, like on your first day here. Galatea asked about me, but you just shut down and took to picking at those scars. Oh, those scars.'

I rubbed the dry area on my elbow. 'You're the one who told me—'

'For all you know, I'm IN YOUR HEAD. I'm **you**...and there's always a choice: jump or live a little longer. Drink the poison that gives you relief or swallow the pain. Sometimes, there is no easy way to live, but it doesn't change. And you're not special,' she spat.

'Are you real?'

'I'm as fake as you are honest.'

'I'm honest,' I hissed through gritted teeth.

'Ooohhh, yeah! Mum loves you, and Daddy didn't bolt the instant they buried my empty casket,' she told me, her eyes wide and mock-innocent, her lies sugar-coated and so obviously false.

'GO AWAY!'

'And you claim to have missed me.'

'Just leave like you always do.'

'I. NEVER. LEAVE. Sure, the voice fades, and my image slips out of your head, but I never leave. From the moment they stole my body, you could hear me there, in the very back of your mind, like an itch you mean to scratch.'

I plugged my ears and slid into the bath, fully clothed. The water was clear, and the gentle *drip-drop-drip* of the tap was relaxing, but she still wouldn't stop.

'They never loved you, not even Axel, the boy you tarnished,'

'I didn't do a thing to him!' I wept, forcing my body to cope with the discomfort of wet clothing.

'You spoiled him. Made him love you when he was manufactured to love me and only me.'

'No!'

'Me. Just me. Only me. He wasn't yours to break.'

Pushing my body down to the bottom of the bathtub was a challenge when all I could hear was her voice, shrill and nasal.

'He never came back because he didn't love you. Even though I know he held your hand and kissed the tears away before he left, you're just baggage. And a boy like him doesn't need to deal with your trauma for you.'

I sank like a toy boat full of water. My body wanted to resist, but I eased my muscles and swallowed the water. Swallowed the pain. Just like she told me to.

'Just phone a hotline or something like that. You don't have to vent to the first person who makes the mistake of treating you with decency.'

My ears twisted her words into pretzels of letters and phonics. Even if I survived, there was nothing for me at home. This institute was just a place of testing, and I had no obligation to fulfil, no reason to stay alive.

So, I'd sink.

It didn't take long for my body to stop fighting the water, but I didn't want to die. I just wanted her to shut up.

'Join me.'

'SHUT UP!' I half gurgled, half vomited.

'Thought you didn't want to die here.'

I didn't, I really didn't, but I couldn't go back to the outside world. It hurt to try to integrate into a society that didn't want me. It was like pushing back against my own nature. And this was my nature: to curl up and die rather than try to get better. It would only hurt for a second but a second was a million years. I couldn't even begin to form words. My ribs felt as if they were stretching to accommodate my bursting lungs. My sternum burned and ached. At least I'd die pretty and young.

The loss of consciousness began to set in, and then nothing worked. It was bad, but I could neither think nor hear the echoes of my twin sister.

It was so sickening to listen to her remnants.

I choked on the only thing around me, and nothing felt quite as good anymore.

The blurry ceiling mosaic was the last thing I saw before things plunged into complete and utter blackness.

The water wasn't even hot.

PART THREE:

A ROCK AND A HARD PLACE

11

Hidden memories resurfaced like skeletons toppling out of the closet as I plummeted into limbo. It was a space betwixt life and death, and I was tearing straight through it. I was falling, but it didn't feel all that real. I was numb to the sensation of the air resistance compressing my feeble human bones into shards. There was a fetid stench of evil and decay in the thick, acrid atmosphere. I closed my eyes, staring at the remnants of bright psychedelic colours and patterns stuck to the insides of my eyelids. As the colours swirled beneath my eyelids, my mind cast back to the sounds Janine had played me in the testing room. 3Yellow had shrouded me in feelings of guilt and 1Red had hit me hard like the death of my sister. Perhaps these sounds were linked to the memories and hallucinations I was having.

For a second, the oxygen drained from my lungs as if I'd been brutally winded.

Before I could comprehend what was happening, my feet found themselves firmly planted on solid ground. The malodour dissipated as if it were nothing more than a patch of bad air, and I felt my muscles simultaneously unclench. I lost consciousness completely. I found my consciousness outside my body. I could see myself, but I wasn't myself, and I couldn't control my movements. All I do is spectate and judge.

I was in the old family car, a 1997 VW with a sun-washed, tea-green exterior, cracked and rusting more by the hour. Like always, I sat in the back, facing the passenger's side window. My face was buried in a brown paper bag, and I was splayed across both of the back seats. Light trickled in from the outside world, illuminating the dust in the small, enclosed area.

The car was completely empty and locked from the inside.

I dropped the brown paper bag and sat up, rubbing my swollen, red eyes, my eyelashes curly and slick with tears.

Only then did I notice my attire.

I was in a grey shirt and a stuffy raven waistcoat, which felt more like a corset. I'd taken my arms out of the sleeves of a matching ebony jacket with peak lapels and wrapped it around my shoulders. My soot-coloured trousers covered the top halves of my patent leather dress shoes that shone in the natural light.

I picked up the paper bag, reached in, grabbed its contents, pulled out a bouquet of velvety black roses and inhaled their delicate, gothic musk.

It was then I remembered the significance of the memory.

The third of March, earlier that year.

The day of the funeral.

I unlocked the door and heaved my body out onto the wet, moss-covered ground, gripping the side of the car to steady myself before going to correct my past wrongdoings. I took two steps forward. Suddenly, I was out of the car park and beside her freshly dug grave.

My mother stood over it, eyes red, her cheeks streaked with running mascara. She hung her head, letting her faded, champagne-blonde hair fall wetly around her face.

I looked at the pearly-white headstone, focusing on every crack and grain of polished sand and found faces in it—faces and things that weren't quite faces, but they weren't quite anything else either. They looked wrong, blended together, melted like hot, burning wax, undressed, rearranged... broken.

I yanked myself out of the trance and back to the matter at hand.

Mourning. It was all that would fill my schedule for the foreseeable future. I would pretend to mourn the girl I'd killed. I searched deep inside myself for even a smidgen of remorse, but found none.

She deserved it. She wanted it. She needed it.

I was the sole child of Tatyana Ostrovsky and Marius N'Goran.

J'étais un enfant unique.

Everything was going to be perfect now.

I looked at my mum inquisitively before approaching her with open arms, ready for an embrace. I hugged her after crossing the grave, not expecting her to return the embrace, but as I rested my chin on her damp, liver-spotted shoulder, I felt her bony arm creep up my back, and I hugged her even tighter.

Then, she gripped the back of my head, seized me by the hair, and dug her fingernails into my scalp.

I bit the inside of my cheek, knowing that if I screamed, she would pull.

'You did this to us. You did this to her,' *my mother said, low and brittle.*

'Mama?' *My voice shook.* 'I didn't—'

'Don't you dare interrupt me, you bastard child. You were the accident; we only ever wanted her.'

'I—'

'I said, don't interrupt me,' she almost yelled, grabbing on even tighter.

I nodded slowly.

'Now, you listen close, and you listen hard, you little сучий. This is all your FAULT, and you know it.' Her face contorted into an image of sheer hatred. 'You wretched brat. You couldn't even get off your arse to pray. I know you did this to her! I KNOW IT! I KNOW IT! I KNOW IT! I KNOW IT! I KNOW—' She screamed through pained sobs and dramatic lamentation, interrupted only by the smell of tobacco and forest fires.

'What the hell do you think you're doing?'

My mother dropped me onto the dry grass, and the sun caught me right in the eye, reflecting off of one of her brooches.

I tried to lift my head, but she kicked me in the face with the toe of her shoe.

I could see my dad in my peripheral vision, dressed in a suit much smarter than, mine with a burnt-out cigarette in his hand.

'There's no point—' said my mother.

'He's coming with me,' my father said with an authoritarian tone.

'He's my child. I RAISED him. You were just there to watch me do it.'

'He's coming with me.'

'No. He's not.' My mother's voice stayed flat and steady. She spoke without a hint of emotion, let alone sadness.

'I don't care what goes down. I just know that by the end of this, we'll be going our separate ways. Either you keep your child, and I send social services to hunt you down, or he comes with me, and you get to live your life.

'Now, give me the car keys.' My dad held out his hand. It was calloused, cracked and dry.

'No. He-h-he's mine. He's mine! HE'S MINE! HE'S MINE!' she replied, yelling and spitting.

'Sammy, get up,' he commanded, speaking directly to me.

I tried to pick myself up despite my weak knees.

'STAY DOWN!'

I wanted to ignore my mother and walk over to my dad, but in the end, I knew she would win the argument, and I would have to deal with the consequences of incurring her wrath.

Still, I got off the floor, resting on my hands because my legs had given out. I stood and began to shuffle toward my father.

'I'M NOT GOING TO LET YOU TAKE HIM!' she screeched, gripping the edges of her hair, ready to tear it all out. 'IF WE GO TO COURT, I'LL GET FULL DAMN CUSTODY, AND YOU KNOW IT!' Her pained screech made me stop dead in my tracks. I didn't want to leave even though I knew that going to a rinky-dink flat bought or rented in a hurry was better than returning to a house so empty that the silence had a sound.

I didn't want to leave her.

'*TATYANA! Stop.*'

I didn't want to leave her.

'Mama, I'll go with you; just please don't scream at me,' I whimpered. My chest constricted, feeling as if I was having an asthma attack.

'SHUT UP!' She tugged my arm, flinging me towards her.

My father stood there, not ready to chase after a grieving mother.

'NEVER CONTACT ME OR MY SON EVER AGAIN!' she said, pulling me along behind her as she walked back to the car park.

I should've just left.

She turned back to me as soon as we were out of earshot. 'You'd better forget his number,' she mumbled, dragging me across the gravel. She threw me onto the floor like a broken rag doll. Black spotted my vision. The holes grew larger and darker until the scene before me shone through the black, nothing more than pinpricks of light on a blank screen.

And then I woke up.

12

I awoke to a new ceiling characterised by incandescent white light. For a moment, before my eyes had adjusted to the light, I thought I'd gone to heaven. But then everything came flooding back and I realised I didn't deserve that. I knew I'd drowned. I knew I'd heard her. I'd heard her again, louder and angrier than ever before. It was a strange sort of parody; I'd nearly died by drowning. Meanwhile, she likely did. I exhaled, feeling the weight of flesh upon my chest, feeling the weight of life, and even then, after my lungs had been voided of water, I didn't feel it a weight I deserved to bear. For a brief moment, I wondered who'd found me. The bathroom door was locked and it looked as if it would have taken tremendous strength to break it down, but, realistically, said person would have simply called for help from the Ospreys, who I presume would have skeleton keys. That said, watching them carry me out must have been traumatic.

That said, where did they carry me to? I sat up and looked around. It looked like the nurse's office at my school; only a curtain was drawn around the bed I was lying in so there might have been more to it. Presumably, we were still within the building. There were no Osprey in the room, but the windows were barred and the sharps bin had a lock on it. I had to admit, whatever evil organisation or pseudo-pharma company had brought us here, they certainly had the budget to do so.

I turned my head to my right where the curtain ended, and saw the ends of a head of ginger hair. I didn't have to guess who it was, but instead of feeling overwhelmingly grateful and filled with joy and love, I felt tired, awful and hungry. I was grateful Galatea had come to wait by my side and I really appreciated it, but knowing her, she'd expect something for it like a medal for being kind to 'Sammy-No-Mates'. My exhaustion was unjust, but her very presence started to mildly piss me off. I chose to ignore it because I really liked her at times and the pros seemed to outweigh the cons.

Behind the curtain, I heard her whispering to someone else. Then, she stood up and pulled the curtain to the side. I took yet another deep breath before preparing to fake the emotions that might hit me right when I saw her face. All of a sudden I forgot about being tired, awful and hungry. Instead, I just sat there and smiled like an idiot. It had just washed over me that she'd been waiting. She had seen my body limp and dead.

I shivered and whispered, 'Thank you,' to her, to myself and to the universe, as I tried to forget the funeral memory.

'You're awake!' Galatea chirped, grinning with all of her teeth.

'It appears so.'

I slid out of the bed. Thankfully, I was still in my own clothes.

Galatea's face fell, and for once, I didn't know why.

'So you're just going to leave?' she asked with furrowed eyebrows.

'Yes,' I stated abruptly. 'Do you want to come with?' I added, not fully getting the point of the question.

'Do you want to come with?' she mumbled to the person behind the curtain. I still didn't understand what was wrong with the question. 'I mean, c'mon Samson. E, emotionally, you may not be the sharpest tool in the shed, but this is foundation.'

'What are you talking about?'

'"Brynhild and I waited for you. I don't know how long exactly, but consider it *all night long...*'

'Yes—agreed.'

'So?'

'So?' I waited for a play-by-play analysis of what I'd done wrong.

'Jesus Christ, Samson, the least you could say is thank you!'

'You didn't have to have a hissy fit!' I bowed my head and mumbled at a just about audible volume. 'Thank you to the both of you for being so considerate.'

Galatea crossed her arms.

'It was *not* a *hissy* fit. I'm only trying to pull you up on your behaviour.'

'I'm sorry, man. I guess it was really inconsiderate of me to drown. Oh, goodness! Gee Wilikers! I guess I'll just have to check in with you before I go through another episode of mental anguish!' I flicked my head up, lifted my hands and slapped them onto my cheeks to mimic an apologetic expression.

'You're not very nice to me. You don't seem to be interested in engaging in casual conversation, *civil* conversation, with me. It makes me wonder why I even bother. Friends are supposed to chat.'

'I honestly don't know if you've noticed, but we've been abducted, and it is all *your* fault, so excuse me if I don't want to engage in *casual* conversation. I have other things on my mind.' I chuckled, astonished at the sheer arrogance she was displaying.

'But I made an effort!'

'You mentioned a name you saw on a *grave* to the person you saw crying at said *grave*. Boy! That's casual conversation if I ever did hear it!' By now, I wasn't just being mildly sarcastic; I was shouting. Only this time, she didn't shout back.

Galatea had hung her head. I could hear sniffling, but her hair covered her face, so I couldn't be sure. 'But I—' she began.

'She's dead! She's…dead,' I said, once to her and once to myself.

She's dead. She can't hurt you anymore.

The partitioning curtain swung to the side, and there was Brynhild sitting in a chair, with a ridiculously thick novel in her hand, her legs crossed, wearing a whole new outfit. This one was still all green, but now it was shorts, a neon tropical shirt, and an ivy-coloured pullover vest.

The novel was titled Анна Каренина, and it was a hardcover, dusty, Saxe-blue volume. Brynhild didn't look particularly interested in it. It was more like she was reading it just to say she'd read it.

She stared blankly at Galatea, gasped, and said, 'Never would've guessed,' shaking her head.

'Shut up, Brynhild,' Galatea and I said in sync.

They stared at each other, Brynhild with deep and ancient hatred and Galatea with an unfounded sense of dread. The tension in the room was thick enough to cut with a knife.

'Thanks, both of you,' I said, using my most plastic smile as I made my way over to the door.

DON'T LEAVE HER!

I slunk out and slammed the door behind me for dramatic effect.

I'd only made it about halfway down the hallway when I heard Galatea plodding after me, so I stopped, hoping for an apology. We were in the small atrium, alone.

Alone once again.

She caught up with me, panting. 'Hey,' she puffed.

'Hello, again.'

She doubled over, trying to catch her breath.

'Samson, I (Damn, I need to walk more) just wanted to say (Omigod, I'm gonna die) that during that—that little tiff, I was absolutely in the right, and you obviously just like to whine and moan to avoid showing other people basic human decency (Kill me, please), but I'm sorry about your sister, and about the fact that I don't respect your boundaries or you, yourself, as a person.'

I raised my eyebrows. 'That was the most half-arsed apology *I have ever* heard.'

Forgive her!

'Yeah, uh…your turn.' She gestured to me, her rust-coloured hair sticking to her face.

Beg her to take you back.

'Okay. Galatea, I'm sorry you need my validation. I am also sorry I've enough self-respect left not to bend over backwards for you. Can we be friends again?'I knew I'd been projecting when I got angry with her. I knew I was actually angry at myself. I'd made a commitment to go through with this but then, when something struck a nerve I waved a white flag without even thinking. I wanted to go through with this, but I didn't know if I could. I didn't know if my mind could take it. I didn't know if I could stomach the pain, even for a second.

'Sure,' she said with a shrug.

That certainly wasn't the reaction I'd expected.

She moved forwards to hug me. Surprisingly, I reciprocated the gesture, and my heart beat faster than it ever had before.

'I was so worried—' she began.

She was worried about you?

'About what?' I asked, resting my chin on her head.

She waved my question away. 'Nothing. I just didn't want to fight with you. You're my only friend here,' she whispered, leaning her head against my chest.

'What about Brynhild or Pygmalion?'

'Brynhild hates me—'

'No, she doesn't—'

'Yes, she does. I know how to judge these types of situations, and Pygmalion is a chaotic neutral who's tilting toward Brynhild. He's also unpredictable. We know next to nothing about him, whereas, in Brynhild's case, we already know she's a smug little bi—'

'Don't talk crap about people behind their backs,' I advised, finding my fingers tangled in her hair. I rushed to pull them out.

'I'm not talking crap,' she scoffed, placing my hand back in her hair.

'Yes. Yes, you are.'

She took a deep breath.

'Fine, let's just walk back to our room and try to find something else to talk about,' she said.

'Sounds GOOD.'

We stood there for a bit. I didn't want to let go, and neither did she. It was a weird and fragile bond that would persevere no matter how many times it frayed.

Galatea sighed. 'I guess we'd better go.'

I let go of her, and she, in turn, did the same.

Right as I pivoted to go upstairs, a strange bell rang. It was like a traditional bell with its reverberating noise and swelling sensation, but the sound itself was different, more delicate.

'What's that?' I queried.

'Aphrodite told me it was the lunch bell.'

'How would *she* know?'

'She skipped the Perception Test and blended in with the floor twos, who'd only done thirty-minute blood tests.'

'To be honest, I didn't notice she was gone.'

'Oh, my God—that's so harsh.' Galatea covered a smile with her hand.

I shook my head, grinning.

She took my hand and walked ahead, leading me. I caught up with her and looked down into her olive-coloured eyes and simply appreciated her. I guess the goosebumps on my skin were better left seen and not spoken. It was an indescribable feeling that almost felt like…like falling in love.

I wondered, if the guilt went, would passion follow?

13

We walked into what seemed to be the lunch hall. The walls were made of beige sandstone, and the floors were marble. It was spotless, making it seem more like a place where important seminars were held than an eating area. There were four tables, long, birch and oriented lengthways, facing a raised black basalt platform with a carved, white lectern planted firmly in the stone. On the left side of the room was a window that spanned the entire wall, displaying the perfectly kept garden outside. There was also a door behind the platform with a window at the top. I assumed the door led to the garden.

It was sunny outside on that particular day.

There were around thirty or so people sitting down at the tables in groups, huddled together like cliques in some coming-of-age, American high school flick.

We sat at the far end of the table nearest the window. There was only one group next to us, with six people in it.

A strawberry blonde girl waved at us, smiling sweetly. She had two gold teeth, one in her lower jaw and the other in her upper right front tooth.

I waved to her.

She turned back to her friends and slid a pair of tangerine-tinted sunglasses onto her face.

'So, what are we supposed to do?' Galatea asked, drumming her fingers on the table.

I shrugged.

No sooner had she finished speaking than the *Griseo Promptu* burst through the door behind the platform, their rigid, monochrome figures pushing through the air. They were carrying paper cups, handing one to every child they passed. It took a while, but finally, they got to us.

A particularly fuzzy-looking person handed me my cup. Inside it was a purple and white capsule.

'My mum told me not to take strange pills,' said the blonde girl rather loudly. She looked back down into the cup. 'Oh well.' She shrugged, tilted her head back, and swallowed the capsule. The *Griseo Promptu* that had given her the cup moved on, going back to the door.

After checking that they were gone, the girl stuck out her tongue to reveal the purple pill with most of its outer colouring rubbed off. She pointed to her mouth and spat the pill into her hand.

I copied her, hiding my capsule under my tongue.

The fuzzy one disappeared, and I spat my capsule into the sleeve of my jumper.

I looked over in her direction to say thank you, but I couldn't seem to find her.

One of her friends had his eyes planted firmly on Galatea. I turned back around, wondering what was catching his eye. My question was answered soon enough.

There, sitting right next to Galatea, was the blonde girl. I realised that her hair wasn't blonde at all but rather a washed-out pink. It was spiked and short, curling around her face like long, aged, rose-coloured thorns. Her cheeks were dimpled and blemished, and her eyelashes were false, thick and black. She swiped her claw-like fingers at me, squinting her mahogany-coloured eyes behind the sunglasses.

'Oh. My. God.' My jaw dropped.

The name that I hadn't been able to place.

'Sylvia—is that you?'

'Heyyy...' She giggled.

It was Syliva Machezelli from my old primary school. I hadn't seen her in years, and honestly, I didn't think I was ever going to see her again. Not that I wanted to.

'Good God, you've grown,' I murmured quietly.

'Fancy seeing you here.' She smirked, drumming her nails on the table.

'Yes, what a coincidence,' I replied, deadpan. 'However did you get here?'

She took off her sunglasses, folded them and slid them into the top of her scarlet camisole.

'Well, I were at Tesco's at night, you know, and I were buying flowers for me mum's birthday. Then, as soon as I got on me bike to start riding home, these funny little dart things kept flyin' past me. Obviously, it was well dark, so I set off, but as you know, I'm not good at ridin' bikes or any of the sporty stuff, even without a tranquiliser lodged in me elbow! Next thing I knew, I were here, being dragged across the dusty floor outside! What 'bout you?'

Galatea and I shared a look. 'Forest,' we said in complete monotonous synchronisation.

'You've changed a lot since last summer,' I stated, grinning.

'You, too. 'Aven't seen yer since Butlin's, but yer've gotten taller!' she exclaimed.

'Sixteen looks good on you.'

'You remembered?'

Galatea stared at us both, looking a teensy bit jealous. 'Hate to break up this…uhh…catch up, but what's going on?'

'We went to the same primary school. My cousin dated her mum for a while. They broke up, her mum started living in a car, and—'

'It's not a car. It's a trailer.'

'It has wheels, it's a car.

'As I was saying, we used to rock up to caravan sites, her mum'd do some scam artist BS, and we'd get wrongfully refunded,' I finished.

'And, the last time I saw yer, you were obsessing over your friend not callin' yer back for three hours.'

'And you said he was probably taking a dump.'

'I stand by that. What was 'is name? Harris…Ben?'

'Otis.'

'Never trust a boy whose name starts with an "O".'

'Yeah, he just wanted to copy my homework.'

'As if yer ever done it!'

At this point, Galatea was visibly peeved. 'My name's Galatea, thanks for asking,' she blurted. 'Don't your *friends* miss you?

'Nah, it's just Beks and Tali.'

'There are six people there,' said Galatea, her eye twitching.

'Beks, Tilly, Trish, Tim and Ash,' Sylvia pointed at each person in turn. 'Wave, Bekah!' she shouted, jolting a girl with a black sixties-style bob and heavy black eyeliner.

Bekah waved frantically.

'So, do you know when the food will arrive?' queried Galatea.

'Last time, it was after the second bell.' Sylvia looked up at a clock I had not noticed before. It was drooping and surreal as if Salvidor Dali had painted it.

'Which is about...' She watched until the long hand hit nine. 'Now.'

The strange bell chimed again. This time, the double doors Galatea and I had walked through flung open, and more *Griseo Promptu* marched in. Instead of cups, they carried plates and silver dishes protected by silver cloches, heading towards a food counter that blended into the walls due to its colour. They laid the plates and dishes on the counter, and an Osprey in purple went around, slapping cutlery and placemats in front of us. They also placed jugs of icy lemon water in the centre of each table and handed everyone a cup. The dishes were then placed equidistant from each other on different sections of the tables.

Sylvia reached for the dish in front of us, a greedy look in her eyes. I slapped her hand away when I heard the click of high heels.

Sure enough, the owner of the shoes appeared soon thereafter.

Madame H.

She hopped onto the raised platform and stood in front of the lectern like a preacher at the start of a sermon, clipped a microphone to her maroon bodice, and cleared her throat. 'Welcome, children. We have decided to name each of the floors after flowers that grow in our very own garden.'

She gestured to the window. 'Please refrain from entering the garden on pain of punishment. Basically, it's off-limits.'

'So, the floor names—floor one shall be named after the radiant kalmia flower and floor two, the beautiful orchid.'

Sylvia rolled her eyes.

'Also, punishment—punishment will be dealt to individuals if they do any of the following: refuse to participate in an examination, assembly or class; deliberately fail an examination or class; use answers or results that are neither theirs nor original; share answers with other participants; disrupt the balance or dynamics of other groups; cause fights or riots; or cause imbalances or problems within their group or any other group,' she explained.

'Do I make myself clear, children?'

'Yesss, Madame H,' said the collective voice of thirty-odd, imprisoned kids.

'GOOD.' She smiled, staying at her post while watching us intently.

'Can we eat now?' Sylvia groaned. 'Honestly, I'm 'aving hunger cramps already.'

'Manners, darling,' I reminded her.

She threw up her hands as if to shrug with the absolute minimum amount of energy possible. Saliva dripped from her bottom lip as she lifted the cloche and looked at what was under it for a moment, not quite understanding what she saw. Then horror replaced perplexity, and she furrowed her eyebrows and recoiled, dropping the cloche in an act of impulse or instinct.

This wasn't normal: Sylvia would have eaten anything if she were hungry enough. Something must've been very, very wrong.

Galatea paled beside her, clenching her jaw as if to stop herself from screaming.

'What? What's wrong?' I asked, spinning the plate towards me, picturing the absolute worst: raw, bloody entrails, splintered human teeth and babies' hands displayed on the plate like a seafood platter.

Compared to what I imagined, the sight before me was relatively tame: it was a pure white rabbit, malnourished and beaten but alive all the same. It was on its back with its limbs tied up with twine and ears stapled to the lettuce it was laid upon. There were dried tomato seeds all over its fur, like fat, yellow ticks. It opened its tiny mouth to cry out but made no sound.

I suddenly realised it had been emitting a low gargling noise. I looked a little closer at it, befuddled by the sound, and found the reason.

Its teeth had been plucked from its gums, leaving nothing but red, bleeding holes to drown itself from the inside. It was absolutely nauseating.

Galatea covered her mouth and lurched forward. She managed to stop herself from retching, but I didn't close the lid, too mesmerised by the wicked sight.

I looked over at Madame H, who was stoic, never daring to break character. She leaned into the microphone. 'Keep calm, children. This is a required procedure. Kill the rabbit, and we might feed you. Respond to this stimuli correctly. Remember that refusal equates to punishment. Thank you, and goodbye.' She strode off the stage as austere as ever.

The saliva in my mouth turned sour.

I must follow orders.

I stood up.

'S-so w-w-which one of us is going to do it?' Galatea stuttered, looking around slowly.

I couldn't turn away. I couldn't answer.

The rules of nature: kill or be killed.

I picked up my knife and ran my thumb against the edge. It was sharp, but was it sharp enough?

It was just an animal.

My eyes darted from the lectern to the rabbit and back again.

It didn't understand.

Only for a moment, I tried to tell it, looking deep into its diseased, pink eyes. *It's only for a moment.*

I raised the knife.

I had the right to live. I had the right to live without guilt.

This was one step.

I faltered for a split second, seeing the ghastly parallels between this proverbial guinea pig and I. I faltered, knowing it also had the same pure right to live.

Kill or be killed; it hurts either way. As I acknowledged this key point, my resolve returned. I tightened my grip on the knife and pointed it towards the rabbit's stomach.

This was the only way.

I slammed my hand down. The knife pierced the rabbit's flesh. I felt the skin on my knuckles stretch and blister.

After all, what *are* morals?

MONSTER!!

I squeezed the handle, forcing it deeper into the small creature, then abruptly withdrew the blade from the body and stepped sideways, away from the geyser of crimson fluid spraying out from the tiny, red-eyed mammal.

Galatea pulled the cloche toward her and vomited violently into it. She wiped her mouth but kept her eyes on my knees. 'Y-you could've g-g-given some warning. Did you think that was for the best?'

This time, I uttered one word in response: 'Euthanasia.' My voice was too cold, too calm and collected. However hard I tried, I couldn't feel scared or outraged. There was only disgust and a sickening sense of self-loathing in my stomach.

For one horrible moment, I wished I were one of the rabbits, slaughtered by a higher power without a second thought.

I gulped down my spit, and with it, all the ghastly thoughts I had a tendency to lose myself in.

A scream reverberated around the hall, and then everything went quiet, shocked into silence by the shrill, abrasive sound.

I looked up to see something worse than what was in front of me.

It was Brynhild, standing two tables away from us. She held her rabbit by the ears and feet, stretched out and vulnerable, facing the ceiling.

'Galatea, don't look,' I heard Sylvia say, her accent breaking.

Brynhild smiled broadly and sighed. It was only a matter of seconds before she'd unhinged her jaw and brought the struggling rabbit closer to her mouth.

I knew exactly what she was going to do.

With shaking hands and a sanguine demeanour, she ripped a bite out of the rabbit's neck. Her eyes glowed a deep carmine as her bestial tendencies arose. Blood dripped down her chin, and the rabbit squealed in pain.

There was a deafening crack, and then it was over.

Scarlet fluid dripped onto her canvas gingham shoes, and I saw her wide, red eyes scan the room, resting dead on my forehead.

She mumbled something inaudibly as she made eye contact with me. Although I couldn't hear it, I felt it in the very marrow of my bones.

I HAD TO DO IT.

I let a shiver pass through my body. Was killing a rabbit really any different than killing my sister? In both cases, I had to do it. Was more death and anguish the answer to simple human remorse?

All that lay in the foreseeable future for me was despair.

I grabbed the rabbit's corpse off of our platter, threw it against the window, and stormed out of the hall, still wielding the be gored knife.

I stepped out into the dark marble corridor, the cold, hard stone clicking under my hardened heels. The air was more breathable outside, where there weren't as many people.

I found a nice, secure wall to collapse against. Somehow, I managed to contort my body into an upright foetal position. I wiped the knife on my jeans and tried to take my mind off of the obscenity I'd committed.

I thought of Galatea and how I felt about her. I tried to use her to calm myself down.

We'd only known each other a short while, and I wanted to know all about her. I wanted to know where she'd been, where she wanted to go, her dreams, her fears and her flaws. I wanted to know everything about her and consume it. I wanted her to be a part of me. I tried to pin down what these people would want from her. I could see Brynhild's inferiority complex and my guilt but I hadn't come face to face with Aphrodite's spite, Pygmalion's anger or Galatea's whatever. If she was one to wear her heart out on her sleeve like I did, then I assumed it'd be jealousy.

The knife slipped, cutting a short, deep gash in my thumb. It stung as the cardinal-coloured liquid rushed out of my skin, slowly dripping onto my white socks.

I pressed my head against my knees.

This was what I deserved.

Nobody could ever even begin to love me. I mean, Axel obviously faked it, and I certainly don't.

'There must be a reason,' I mumbled.

I heard light, fleeting footsteps on my left. The person was likely running or hopping from side to side to avoid putting too much weight on their lower half. I lifted my head and looked up, shifting my gaze to see Aphrodite barrelling down the hallway barefoot.

It was as if she were standing still but moving at near-light speed. She juddered to a halt when she drew near.

'Good afternoon,' I said, nodding as I wiped my bleeding thumb on my trousers.

'Because of you, there's nothing "good" about it,' she droned as she strode towards me.

'I'm sorry,' I began, pulling myself up from my sitting position.

She put her hand on my shoulder and pinched with all five of her fingers. 'Stay down.'

I slid back down, just as she'd commanded.

'And give me the knife.' She extended her free hand, indicating that I should place the knife in it.

I dropped it in her palm, and she flipped it around her fingers, eventually holding it with her ring and pinky fingers. 'Stop sulking. You've been through the same ordeal as most people here, but with the way you've acted, you're going to get us all killed. Suck it up, okay?' she berated me, staring deep into my eyes with her own caliginous orbs.

'What have I done wro—'

Aphrodite rolled the knife back to her thumb and held it against my cheek. 'The world doesn't revolve around you. And you know full well what you've done. I get that it takes deeper emotions like yours a bit of extra time, but stop sulking.'

She inhaled through gritted teeth, pressing the serrated edge against my flesh. 'You can keep thinking the *sun* shines out of your arse, but maybe consider that having a little fit here isn't as inconsequential as it is in the real world.' Grinning sardonically, she grazed my cheek.

She was so close I could smell her: the scent of copper, burnt hair, tobacco and strawberry shortcake.

It made me sick.

'They're helping us. I'll tell you what I told Brynhild: you can't win without knowing how to play, but this is less of a board game and more of a sport. By dying, you, individually, would've messed up the arrangement. There's more than you think resting on your shoulders, Atlas,' she spat, her lips dry and cracked.

I grabbed the wrist wielding the knife. 'You said at the very beginning, you and Pygmalion; you said they'd make us "inhuman",' I speculated, prying her hand away from my face.

Aphrodite forced it back down, pinching my shoulder harder than ever. She glared at me with crepuscular eyes like charcoal smudged on tea-stained acrylic paper. She had a threatening sort of aura that extended far from her body. It made her seem domineering and large, with a hint of tenebrosity.

"Fraid of being cut, *pretty* boy? This isn't about being inhuman. This is about you. Get your shit together. Are you in or are you out? If one of us kicks it, it'll upturn the entire project. If you *die*, either by my hand or your own, this whole thing goes up in smoke.

'You may not have anything to live for but I for one want to live to be *perfect*. I need these tests in order to be *perfect*. I'll have no evil and no mortal tendencies. I'll be an angel, you know. Better yet, I'll be a *God*.' She shook her head and sighed. 'I know you don't want this; you just know it's for the greater good, but if your heart isn't in it…honestly, you're better off *escaping*. 'S no easy task. This place is built and secured like Alcatraz, but I think you'll work something out *event*ually.

'But before you *leap* out of a second-floor window, think of Galatea or Pygmalion. Do you really want them to die because you're too spiteful, too weak to live?' Aphrodite let go of me, withdrawing the knife with a sharp look and a maniacal giggle. She strutted a reasonable distance away before turning back and mouthing, '*DON'T SCREW THIS UP*.'

I felt a sting on my cheek, a bruise on my shoulder and a shiver running its course down my spine. Maybe there was some truth in what she'd said after all. My heart wasn't in it. I wasn't even thinking about the big picture, but now I would.

14

Begrudgingly, I turned to face the door, ready to re-enter the dining hall. First, I pressed my hand against the Daedalian teak wood door, absorbing the vibrations from even the tiniest worm to the heavy, thunderous footsteps of the Ospreys in their steampunk steel-toed boots.

I took a deep breath and slunk into the room, trying to be as inconspicuous as I could manage. I crossed the hall, taking big, powerful strides that echoed ever so slightly. It was too quiet. When I'd left, it looked as if the scene was about to descend into absolute chaos, but now the room was perfectly silent. The thick, goopy atmosphere was barely even marred by the few whispers here and there.

I bowed my head and hid behind my hair until I reached the table by the window. The bloodstains on the glass had been cleaned, unlike the ones on the floor, but the lifeless cadaver of that poor creature remained, still twitching post-mortem.

I could see my vivid reflection in its glassy, dead eyes. They were so small and marble-like, filled with the residuum of long-gone hope. I felt those uncomfortable sensations: the bat missing its target, the itch inside my heart, the boulder in my stomach.

I linked my malaise to the audio track I'd heard in Janine's office and felt violently ill all of a sudden.

Goosebumps arose on my arms, making my hair stand on end. I perceived at least thirty pairs of eyeballs boring into my skin and sat abruptly down, choosing the seat at the very end of the table.

When I managed to direct my wandering eyes to the front of the room, I caught a soggy, depressing stare from Galatea. Her eyebrows were furrowed, and those beautiful green eyes had turned a dark stormy grey, crinkled at the edges as if it hurt to look at me.

I took another deep breath.

At least I can't disappoint her anymore.

An Osprey barged through the back door, power walking in their clanky metal boots. This person's cloak was bone-white, the edges tinged with mould and dried blood. They wore a black leather plague doctor's mask, and a hemmed black tophat with a blue velvet ribbon wrapped around it.

They stepped up onto the platform, parked themselves behind the lectern, adjusted the microphone, and dusted off their cloak with gloved hands as the other Osprey—in red cloaks—filed in from another door beside the rostrum. They were like an orderly, uniform stampede.

All the while, the person in white clapped. Their sweaty, vinyl gloves made a gross, sticky sort of noise when they separated.

Soon, the sound of heavy, stumbling feet died down, and the room fell completely quiet, save for the repetitive sticking and unsticking of the gloves. Then, they rolled back their baggy sleeves, peeled off the gloves and breathed heavily into the microphone. After that, they took off their mask with its long, spindly skeletal fingers, whiter than virgin snow. The top hatfell off, landing next to the microphone on top of the lectern.

The first thing that was revealed was a mess of flaxen hair that looked as if it'd been shorn off at least two years ago. Glasses tinted blue rested on their thick nose bridge, leading down to a hooked, freckled nub of a nose. Behind those glasses were eyes as unfathomable as the contents of space and pupils as vast as the unexplored world under the sea.

Finally, they placed the mask beside the hat and gloves, tapped the microphone, and cleared their throat.

Like the other unmasked Osprey I'd seen, they looked fairly young, like early twenties—and I mean VERY early twenties. They pursed their maroon-painted lips, pausing only to wipe a bit of smeared lipstick off of their chin and scratch their sharp, masculine jawline.

'Thank you, everyone, for waiting,' he said softly into the microphone, poking their sharp cheekbones with a pearly, dead finger.

'I am Dr Ivanov, head osprey of this particular division. We usually call head Ospreys…ummmmmmm…ummm…' he snapped his fingers and furrowed his eyebrows as if the word he was thinking of long, smart and complex.

'черт возьми[6]…*иттт*…Эврика![7] That is it! Buzzards.'He spoke with a neutrally Slavic accent that

---

[6] CHERT VOZ'MI = Damn it.
[7] EVRIKA = Eureka.

reminded me of my mother's, though hers was more aggressively Belarusian.

I felt the hairs on the back of my neck prickle, the absence of my mother's grasp like a phantom itch.

'Buzzards like myself are in charge of little off-the-book trials like the one you have all just gone through.

'Speaking of trials, I would like to congratulate those of you who were able to complete the simple task laid before you. Please stand up if you managed to neutralise the rabbit.'

I rose slowly from my seat, my knees knocking In the corner of my eye, I saw Brynhild push the table away so she could stand on the bench. Beside her, Pygmalion stood up timidly, slumping his shoulders as if he'd just lost a custody battle. His eyes met mine, and they seemed to hiss words of warning.

The Buzzard clapped, calm and sardonic at first, then enthusiastic and loud when they were joined by their underlings. The hall echoed with synchronised claps and fake raucous cheering.

'Extremely well done, all of you.' The Buzzard contorted their face into a gnarly, grotesque grimace as they glowered back at the sea of seated children.

I looked at Galatea and Sylvia, indicating they should stand up. The latter of the two exhaled in relief, the colour flushing back to her face, while the former couldn't even meet my gaze. My heart bled as I desperately tried to find something in her eyes beyond the pain and trauma.

She turned her head away from me, and in the short half a second that I'd caught her eye, everything on her face, from the scars on her chin to the freckles on her forehead, told me she expected more of me or that I'd betrayed whatever faith she was stupid enough to have in me.

Tears boiled behind my eyes as I balled up my fists, digging my nails into my palms to stop myself from crying. I clenched my jaw and swallowed, pushing back the hopelessness.

I didn't know what to think or how to feel because every time I so much as squinted, I saw a phantasmagoria of misery formed by my tears, flashes of scenarios in my mind, playing like a broken record dragging on the same groove for all of eternity. I saw her face shredded, ripped and mauled by wolves, a bloated corpse with ginger hair, ready to burst in the middle of the street, a broken body at the foot of a skyscraper, and worst of all, her telling me that she didn't want to be around me anymore.

I shuddered, my skin practically leaping off of my bones and stumbled to the front, tripping over my own feet like a total klutz. When I arrived on the platform, after pushing through clumps of regular Ospreys, I hung my head in shame, not bearing to make eye contact with anyone in the audience.

'And now, those of you who thought the rules didn't apply to you—you thought you could slither on by, coasting on the inertia of those who completed the task successfully, didn't you? Well, Вы являетесь собственностью компании. Ваш выбор и мораль недействительны,[8]' said the Buzzard, their nose twitching as if they were experiencing a foul smell.

---

[8] You are the property of the company. Your choices and morals are invalid..

Some of the Russian words they used were familiar to me as I'd heard my mother screaming them on the phone at some time or another.

All I could make sense of were the words 'company property' and 'invalid', though I was sure they'd become clear with context.

'The moment you arrived here, you all forfeited your autonomy. I don't care if any of this goes against your moral philosophy—you do as you're told and don't question. Madame Hortense was kind enough to tell you exactly what would happen if you disobeyed direct orders. This was a conscious decision you made to be defiant, and for that you'll need to be punished...'

They kept talking, but the words only fused with the slow, steady rattle of the vent just above their head.

I took a gander at the vent, conscious of how many people were watching me. It was human-sized, rusty and built into the wall. The sound it made was raspy and hollow, implying a tunnel about a foot wide, almost exactly like the size of the vent covering. The screws on the covering were fairly loose-looking, and one of them was missing altogether. The breeze coming from the vent was extremely faint, hinting at a fan much, much farther down. It suggested a possible connection between this vent and other ones. I sieved through my memory, trying to recall if I'd seen another fan like it anywhere else.

Come to think of it, Janine's office had one. At the time, I hadn't noticed it because it was functioning perfectly.

What was it Aphrodite had said? 'You'll work something out *eventually*...'

I felt an escape plan forming in my head.

I nudged Sylvia discreetly to get her attention. When I knew that she was listening, I bent down and mumbled the outline of my plan into her ear.

She slowly looked round at me and bit her lip as if thinking. 'So, whaddya want me to do?' she whispered back.

'I'm going to need you to collect anything sharp and pointy you can find—do you know how to make a shiv?'[9]

'Maybe. I mean, yeah. Anything else?'

'Can you make a mental note of every room you go into that has a vent? If you can't manage that, just focus on the collecting, and I'll get someone else to do it,' I whispered, turning away.

'I'll try.'

'Thank you.'

I zoned back in time to hear what the Buzzard had to say about punishment. 'The Orchid group will have their punishment session first, commencing a single day from now. The Kalmias will have theirs an hour after. You will be punished in alphabetical order, taking place downstairs at the chime of the second bell. The second bell is different from the lunch one. I can't explain how, but you'll know it when you hear it.

'When you do hear it, proceed to the hallway just outside the assembly hall. An Osprey will lead you down. If you've completed the task today, attendance is optional but recommended. This means that you may or may not have a free period.

---

[9] A makeshift knife-like object.

'Thank you for your attention.' They put their mask back on and tucked their gloves into the top hat before staggering off-stage like a drunk.

A lesser Osprey marched onto the stage. 'Dismissed!' she said, her voice shrill, high-pitched and grumpy. She made a shooing motion with her hands. 'The two groups will merge for this examination. Follow the *Griseo Promptu* to the next room for DNA and bacterial testing.'

I hopped off the rostrum and fell into the slow, worm-like line behind Pygmalion. Walking slightly ahead, I fell into place beside him. 'Hi,' I greeted him softly, not using my regular abrasive tone. 'So, I know we haven't exactly been the best of friends—' I cut myself off, checking that I'd gotten his attention.

'You need a favour?' He stopped and stared at me with his eyebrow raised.

My heart caught in my throat, and I felt copious amounts of blood fill my cheeks.

Remember what Dad said about bullies? They can smell fear.

I exhaled heavily. 'Oh, thank God. You understand, right?'

'Why would *I* help *you*?'

My entire body froze.

'I—I've—I've got this plan to y-y-you know...umm... escape,' I stuttered, trying to talk with a completely dry mouth.

'And?'

'I was wondering if you wanted to come and scout ahead.'

'I think I understand. You want me to be a *canary*, an expendable, yeah?' He raised his eyebrow higher.

'You could do some other stuff, too,' I exclaimed feebly, shrinking into my jumper.

'Like what?'

'I need somebody to blueprint all the rooms with vents in them. I need *you* to blueprint the vents and take notes on how the building operates and…umm…stuff.' I blushed harder, the tips of my ears boiling.

We crossed a courtyard I'd never seen before, with a beautifully carved sandstone fountain as the centrepiece. Grass peaked through the brownish tiles, susurrating in the abrasive wind.

'Okay. I'll do the second thing, but I need you to do something for me.'

I licked my lips. 'Of course. Anything you want.'

'I'll talk to you. We'll work things out then,' he said, not even making eye contact with me. With that, he disappeared to run off to his merry murderess in green, leaving me at the very back of the line.

As he left, I caught a glance at a white, plastic vent cover. This one was a bit smaller than the other one, but it was large enough for a petite, flexible person to wriggle through it if they really tried. If the vents were connected to the courtyard, they must also be connected to other spaces on the property.

My plan was developing by the minute.

There were only two more people to convince before I could put my plan into action, but it was unlikely either of them would agree.

I watched the sterile glass syringe sink into the crook of my elbow without a word. Blood gushed from my vein like water from a punctured hose. It sloshed around inside the barrel and dripped from the needle.

The person taking my blood sample was in a rough, leather bird mask that stopped just below their nose. Their mouth was covered by a surgical one, blue to match their scrubs.

The chair I was sitting in was a red, retro-American diner-type swivel stool.

It took all the self-control I had not to spin myself silly.

The room was high-ceilinged and cavernous, filled with monitors, computers, cameras and all sorts of scary-looking machines.

I heard the chair on my right squeak as its inhabitant swivelled sluggishly around and tilted my head to see Brynhild with dried blood on her clothing, laying across the chair like a child who'd just come down from an extreme sugar-high.

My knee-jerk reaction was to shrivel my nose in disgust, but I refrained from making another enemy and put on my casual poker face.

'I can hear your bones,' she whispered, smiling like a Cheshire cat. She continued to turn in a full circle, accelerating her spinning speed and kicking the person trying to take her blood sample with long, knobbly-kneed legs.

'You know, I'd look good with blue eyes,' Brynhild announced, slurring her words together in a mess of Germanicmispronunciation. She then tugged angrily at herpigtails.

'So,' she began, turning to me. 'I've been wanting to give myself *ein* pixie cut. I think it'll make me look super hot, but I'm interested to hear what you think.'

'Oh, well—' I choked on my own saliva, surprised by her sudden burst of energy.

'Doesn't matter. *Fick dich ins knie.* I'LL DO IT ANYWAY!' From her attitude, she was probably still a little sugar-high.

'Are you…okay?' I wondered, watching her spin herself into oblivion.

'Why wouldn't I be?' they stopped and grinned at me with yellowing teeth shielded by a burned retainer stained with blood, plaque, tea and a mysterious purple liquid.

'No—no reason,' I whimpered, moving away from the stench of rotting meat wafting from her mouth.

'Wait! I need your opinion on hair. I now realise that pixie cuts are stupid, and I should *stattdessen* get a short…as you call it…pageboy cut. I think it'd look cute on me. Don't you agree?' she asked, undoing one of her scruffy plaits.

'O-okay? Anyway, Brynhild, I have a job for you.' I whispered so I wouldn't be overheard by the Osprey next to me.

'Noooooooo…not a job!' she slumped sideways in the chair, flapping her slim feet at the Osprey beside her.

I felt a different needle prick my arm. This time, I was being injected. 'Trust me. It'll be real easy,' I whispered, wincing.

'Blahhhhhhhhhhh. Okay!' She grinned, going cross-eyed as she tried to stare at me while upside down.

'Sometime soon, either this week, next week or the one after, when we're in the dining hall, I want you to sit opposite me. After the second bell, I'll give you a signal. I'll knock three times on the table. When you receive the signal, I want you to cause a scene: chuck plates, scream at the top of your lungs, bite people, whatever feels right.'

'And why do you want me to do that?' she asked, staring dreamily into my eyes.

'Well, while you're raising hell, a group will slip out of the dining hall and into the nearest vent—'

Brynhild cut me off, snapping at me as if I'd just killed her Tamagotchi. 'You're leaving me behind?'

'Not necessarily. You'll also have a way out. You'll continue to cause havoc until you make such a mess that the attention slips off of you and onto the destruction you've caused. While everyone's distracted, you'll run through the off-limits garden, into the turret of the testing facilities block (the one we're in right now), find an open vent, climb into it and crawl toward the light.' I took a breath. 'Do you understand?'

'I can taste your eye colour. It tastes like carbon monoxide, but that's okayyyyy…' She trailed off, eyes glazing over and going foggy as she stared at something right by my foot.

'Do you understand?' I repeated myself.

'Totally.' She giggled, slipping out of her chair and onto the floor. She rolled around on the ground for a bit, getting all sorts of gross debris in her platinum-blonde hair.

I finally turned away from the train wreck to face the biggest monitor in the room. It had the flattest screen I'd ever seen, and it was displaying a still message written in yellow on a cyan-blue background.

At the bottom of the screen, it had the time and date: 13:59 02/11/2005

The date was wrong, wasn't it?

Oh, God.

Galatea told me I'd been unconscious for a few hours, and I'd gone under on the twenty-third, after my second visual examination.

Did she—

Have I—

I'd missed it. The day she'd died. The days had blurred together so much that more than a week had passed.

My stomach churned. I blinked and squeezed my eyelids tightly together before reading the bulky paragraph of text above the date.

```
First, your blood sample will be taken
by one of our medical professionals.
This  blood  sample  will  be  tested
to see if it is compatible with a
certain strain of bacteria we have
been  testing.  Ultimately,  it  is
harmless…in theory.

Next,  you  will  be  injected  with  a
different substance. This is another
bacterium dubbed 'усилитель' by one
of our senior Buzzards. It is also
```

```
known as 'STAGE 1', and it is meant
to serve as a base treatment. It
will help you complete future
examinations to the best of your
abilities. This procedure is almost
absolutely safe.

It is also mandatory.

From
Madame A. Hortense.
```

I looked over at my arm. There was a five-millilitre syringe sticking out of a throbbing, blue vein underneath my thin, tensed skin. It was almost empty, with a residual fluid coating the bottom, clumping together in green, putrid lumps like curdled milk. I retched and yanked it out of my arm, feeling my muscles tense and constrict. My fingers twitched involuntarily like the deceased cadaver of a flesh-coloured crab. In a similar fashion, my eyelids slid down over my eyes as if I had ptosis. One of them was more droopy than the other, partially obstructing my vision. As I desperately tried to hold my fingers still, I was overcome with an overwhelming urge to scratch the red fluid-filled bump forming where I'd removed the needle. My breath caught in my throat, the oxygen refusing to reach my lungs. In my chest, my heart palpitated, throbbing in syncopated time. My head felt as if it were pulsing, matching the beat of my fluttering heart. In fact, it wasn't fluttering at all. It was pulsating, vibrating and halting dead in its beats for seconds at a time.

The bump had swollen, morphing into a fat, purulent whitehead before my very eyes. Gagging slightly, I stuck the nail of my index finger into the middle of the inflamed spot and watched a semi-solid, yellow substance spill out of the thin layer of red skin that had previously protected it. The deposition of pus made my entire body tingle unpleasantly. The sound of skin splitting open turned my saliva thick and slackened my jaw.

The Osprey by my side had been gone for a while now. Come to think of it, I couldn't see anyone in scrubs around the room. I swallowed the acid rising in my throat and took a quick survey of the room. There was a large overhead ventilation pipe with open spaces every half a metre or so. The metal holding it up was almost entirely reflective, showing an inverted image of the grey polycarbonate walls. The network of pipes above also caught the light from the monitors, which had changed since I'd last looked. The note continued…

It takes a while for your bloodstream to accept the booster, so you shall be dismissed in 00:08:10s. It will only take five more minutes for the spasms to calm down, and you will need another five to ensure you are still in control of your motor functions. After you are dismissed, the ensuing side effects will vary for each and every one of you. Some of you may not experience any at all.

Side effects?! I thought I was just having a dime-a-dozen convulsion. And what was 'to make sure you are still in control of your motor functions' supposed to mean?

I sighed and calmed my twitching body parts using the same technique I'd use to control my panic attacks. I took a long, deep breath and stopped the tremors. I flexed my fingers, batted my eyelids and wiggled my toes.

I was perfectly fine.

Nothing mattered.

Tomorrow would be a new day.

I'm in a bad place, but everything will work out.

I jumped off of the stool. There were only seven more minutes and thirty more seconds to go.

I walked over to Sylvia, who was scratching her nose absent-mindedly. 'Aloha,' she said whimsically, wiggling her fingers.

'I don't speak Spanish.'

'I said, "Aloha".' She chewed on the left temple of her gold-framed sunglasses.

'And I said, "*me no hablo español*".'

'M'kay...what do you want?'

'Uhhhhhh...' I counted the items in my list on my fingers. 'Camaraderie...a-a-anxiolytics. Ummm...uhhh....' I made a hissing noise as I sucked in air through my gritted teeth. I had something I genuinely needed from her, but I couldn't for the life of me remember what. Was I just there to kill time, or did I have something to say?

'What do you want *from me*?' She giggled.

I clicked my fingers, desperately trying to hold onto the train of thought that was swiftly leaving the station.

Oh, yeah! The apology!

'Uhhhhhhhhhh…do you know how I might apologise to Galatea?' I queried, almost begging for advice.

'I-I dunno why you'd wanna do that. I mean, she doesn't seem angry. Maybe that's just her resting face.' Sylvia slid her glasses from the top of her head and pushed them onto her face.

'Well, it's not. We've been arguing quite a lot today, and she looked absolutely shattered when I killed the rabbit.'

'She's gotta understand. It's just business. If you 'adn't done it, we'd be in for something horrible with the others,' my friend reasoned while checking that her falsies were secure.

'I know, but I think the girl deserves an apology. She sat in the infirmary with me for however long when I…when I…when I…when I…got into some *trouble*. Also, I can't afford to disagree with her. It'd jeopardise the whole plan,' I explained.

'Then don't disagree with her. You can apologise, but you don't have to mean it. Do what you have to do, babes. Just because you're an attention seeker doesn't mean she is, too.'

'But she'll KNOW!' I hissed.

'You know what they say: hurt people hurt people.'

'You have no idea what you're talking about, do you?'

'Nope.'

'And you just thought the words sounded nice coming out of your mouth, didn't you?'

'Yep.' She coughed into her lap. 'And it's that easy to apologise to people. Just say groovy-sounding words that feel nice on your tongue. That's all the English language is, anyway. You think Winston Churchill is one of the most beloved prime ministers in all of history because actions speak louder than words?'

'Yeah—'

'No, it was because he made good mouth sounds, I mean, "We will fight them on the beaches"? The greatest mouth sound of all!'

I sighed. 'I'm surprised you know who he is.'

'And I'm surprised you haven't run your fluffy little tush outside yet! Go!'

'But we still have five more minutes. What if I have a seizure?'

'Then I guess you might die.' She spun me around and shoved me toward the exit with her fake tan-stained hands.

An awkward sort of alarm, like a classic school bell, rang out through the halls. I left my spot by the door and blended in with the crowd of people exiting the room. The squirming, writhing mass of people enveloped and carried me across the network of buildings as I prepared my apology.

When we had reached the atrium, the crowd had dissipated, leaving an orderly two-by-two line.

I spotted her in the corridor: ginger hair, yellow dress. She was talking to some girl I didn't know, the girl from earlier, the one with the blue hair.

I could only partially hear them chat.

'I'm so glad I found you. I just keep butting horns with everyone in my room,' Galatea gushed, her voice rising and falling with her regular East London lilt.

'I know what you mean. It's getting a bit scary now.'

They turned their heads to share a sympathetic look, and I got a better view of the other girl's face. She had short, curly, black eyelashes that scraped her sharp, arched eyebrows. There were scratches and old, misshapen bite marks on her neck, presumably from a small rodent or a cat.

They came to the split staircase and said their goodbyes. The other girl scratched her ear and grinned. 'I'm Talia, by-the-by.'

'Galatea.'

Talia ran up the stairs, hopping like a hyperactive kangaroo. On the other side of the same staircase, Galatea dragged her feet from marble step to marble step with less motivation than a melancholic tortoise.

I thought this would be the perfect time to apologise.

I caught up with her, which was surprisingly hard, considering how lethargically slow she seemed to be.

'Hey, Tea…can we talk?' I mumbled, continuing tentatively.

'Oh, so we're doing pet names now?' She gasped overdramatically. 'The double standards.'

'Sorry.'

'Gosh, golly, no! Don't apologise. The great Samson never apologises!'

'Galatea–'

She rolled her eyes, and I internally screamed.

'Galatea, I just want to talk.'

'Let me guess: it's all about you. You don't actually care about anything I have to say, and even if you did, you wouldn't take anything I said to heart because you're a little *bitch*.' She listed her points on her fingers and then smiled mawkishly, squinting like a toad. She swung from side to side in a mock-cutesy fashion.

'Or…or is this like the conversation we had earlier, where I ask for the bare GODDAMN minimum from you, but you're too stubborn to even say a simple *thank you*?' She giggled manically.

I couldn't get a word in edgeways.

'Oh, deary, I could say so much in very few words. If we had a brief five-second conversation about me, you'd learn more than you ever cared to ASK. Maybe I could educate you on my vegetarianism. Maybe I could guide you to the light but Go-God didn't put me here to guide you to the light; He put me here because He hates my GUTS!' she shrieked during fits of uncontrollable laughter.

'And don't you dare call me crazy 'cause I'm not complicated! I'm not! And I'm way more DAMN SANE THAN YOU!'

Her voice shook the room, rumbling as it tumbled down the stairs.

That's how you know she's angry.

'I'm sorry.'

'Oh, my God! I'm not your girlfriend. I'm not Jesus. I need a real apology, sunshine!'

She put her finger on her lip in the same mock-cutesy manner she'd demonstrated earlier.

Even if she accepts your apology, she'll still hold a grudge.

I looked around. The hallway was empty.

'Okay, I've been a bit in my own head lately… aaaannnndd…' I walked up the stairs until I was a step below her, and I could see into her suddenly dark eyes.

'I recognise I've got an inflated sense of my own importance, and I have not taken other people's thoughts, feelings and-slash-or opinions into account. I realise that I don't know you, and I think I'd like to. Can we start afresh?'

Really? A textbook apology?

She raised her eyebrows. 'I don't think that's going to cut it, sweetheart.'

I must admit, I was a bit taken aback by this refusal. 'Well then, what will?'

'You need to agree to my T's & C's.'

'Like a list of demands?'

'Perhaps. Think of it more as an exchange. I'll be dumb and blindly follow you to hell if you do what I want.'

I exhaled heavily. 'What could you possibly want from me?'

'R-E-S-P-E-C-T. If you want our arrangement—'

'Arrangement?'

'Friendship. If you want our friendship to go back to the way it was before, you need to show me that you respect my choices, my beliefs and myself. I know I'm not posh, and I don't speak as eloquently as you, but that doesn't mean I matter any less. You can start by asking for my opinion on things, even if it's not what you want to hear. Chances are, I have better judgement—'

'Absolutely. I agree to Galatea Owens' terms and conditions—'

'I wasn't finished.'

I waited for her to continue.

'Well, actually, I was,' she admitted, looking rather ticked off. 'I can't really think of anything right now, but when you next mess up, I'll add stuff to my list. Do you have anything you need to say?'

'No, not really.'

'So, do you?'

'Ohh…okay,' I reluctantly agreed.

She grinned, triumphant, and then she eyed me up. It must've been a full minute that we stood there without a word.

'Lord, what do you want from me now?' she sighed, the corner of her mouth perking up.

'I don't,' I began, taken aback by her abrasive, grating tone.

'I'm kind, not stupid.' She giggled, 'You know, one of these days, we need to have a good and proper chinwag.'

'It's not really a favour. I just want you to…' I pulled her shoulder toward me slightly so I could whisper in her ear. 'I want you to escape with me,' I murmured, feeling her delicate, flaky skin brush my cheek.

'WHAT?' She stumbled and fell as she leapt back.

'We can talk about the specifics later, but I just want to make sure you're in. You are in, right?'

'I-I-I…Of course!'

I nodded and stepped aside, ascending the stairs, holding onto the stone banister.

<h1 style="text-align:center">15</h1>

Sleep wouldn't come to me. I stood over Galatea's bed, gazing out of the window. I looked down at her. Her hair was knotted over her face, curling tightly around her neck like auburn snakes weaving themselves into a noose.

The moon peeked in, shrouded partially by wisteria-coloured clouds. I gazed up at it and felt it pulling me in, whispering to me, luring me to it like a moth to a porch light. It was bright and luminous but waning all the same. It drenched the room in a silver, celestial glow. It was as if the shimmering light made every item in the room slightly less canny, from the disproportionate furniture of the level above to the broken bathroom door knocked off its hinges. The hearth was briefly alight with the very memory of flames dancing across the charcoal, illuminating the faces of willing lodgers or wayward nuns from the past as their voices bounced off the walls. I breathed in the air, not of a prison room but of a place with untold tales and forgotten history.

For a moment—just for a moment—I could sense the building breathing. It groaned and creaked like a living entity, alive but only just, like a fresh wound with hints of infection.

I closed the large window, crossed the room, and crawled back into my bed. Above the bed was a vent, the same as the one in the dining hall. Tonight, the vent was off, and I only heard the squeak of rats as opposed to the regular mechanic huffing. I tried to get into the ideal sleeping position and felt a lump underneath the mattress cover. Beneath the sheet was something wrapped in fabric and secured with a broken hairband. I picked it up, perplexed.

Who could have left it for me?

There was more than one thing in the package; it was a bundle of various small objects. At first, I wasn't going to open it, but then my curiosity got the better of me. I ripped the hair tie off of the fabric and watched it unfurl. When the first layer of fabric came off, I realised that it was a torn piece of a shower curtain. The second layer was part of a pillowcase, and the final was a jaggedly cut corner of a damp purple hand towel.

The package also contained the sharp objects I'd asked Sylvia for earlier: screws, hairpins and even needles from the medical bin. At the very bottom was a note written in red on the back of some screwed-up newspaper. When I picked it up, it wasn't light enough to be just a piece of paper, and I felt something concealed in it.

The bright red scrawl on the back was clearly in Sylvia's handwriting. It read::

i dont know what ur gonna do with this, but i trust u to make decisions that will help people.

USE WITH CARE.

I opened the newspaper, and a toothbrush with its bristles cut short, fell out. For a second, I thought Sylvia was playing tricks on me with her warped sense of humour, but then I saw the edge.

It was razor sharp.

This wasn't a joke anymore.

With that, you could kill.

You could kill again.

I wrapped the package back up and hid it under my pillow because I didn't think anyone would come into the room while we were out.

What have you done?

It was suddenly all so real.

What are you going to do?

The events of the past year washed over me.

Somebody died.

I'd been abducted, and we were going to escape.

How?

How are you going to do it?

I lay down and gazed at the popcorn-textured ceiling. My eyes started to droop the very second I began fleshing out my plan.

An ear-splitting noise brought me to my senses.

'Samson? Samson?' Janine was calling my name and snapping her fingers at me. The room came back into focus, and I noticed the picture she was waving at me.

'Sorry,' I said with a sigh.

'It's fine. What do you think this picture is? What emotions does it convey? Why was it taken?' she asked, holding up a negative Polaroid of some poppies in a field. The shot was slightly off-centre, focusing on something in the mid-ground.

My mind raced, searching for answers in the obscure yet basic photograph.

Then, I stopped.

I didn't have to do this.

'Janine? Do you *enjoy* your job, Janine?' I enquired, my eyes firmly planted on the vent in the corner of the room. 'Do you?'

She furrowed her brow and looked at me with a queer expression. 'That's not very releva–' she began, smiling awkwardly and scratching the back of her head.

'Do you enjoy it?'

'Well, yes.' She nodded and checked her antique wristwatch, fidgeting and twitching ever so slightly as if she were sitting upon an anthill.

I continued to pry. 'So, you enjoy examining the minds of abducted kids, minors not taken with parental or guardian consent. Abducted. You enjoy it, do you?'

'Ye–'

'How old are you, Janine?' Like the Buzzard, she didn't look a day over twenty. It seemed as if my line of questioning had found a weakness.

'That isn't quite appropriate for me to–' her eyes darted around the room, trying to segue back into the photos, 'to disclose.'

'How old are you?' I asked, louder this time.

She scratched the back of her neck and mumbled something that sounded vaguely like, 'Well, if you must…

'I am twenty-nine,' she finally said, her voice trembling and cracking on the worst possible notes.

She was obviously lying.

'How old?' I uncrossed my legs and leaned forward.

'Twenty-five.' Beads of sweat formed just below her hairline.

'HOW OLD?' I slammed my hands down on the table.

'Nineteen! Gosh! I-I-I-' She sighed and her lip began to quiver. 'You don't understand.'

'Explain then. Enlighten me." I'd struck gold. I'd get answers. I'd be able to leave with nothing on my chest but what I entered with.

'You know about the experiment, right?' she asked.

'Of course I do.'

'I mean, do you really know?'

At this, I sat down.

'What do you mean?'

'This isn't just to do with emotions. This isn't some little experiment, just for fun, just to see what will happen. We're going to be put to use—"

I understood what Aphrodite had said before. '"*War is coming if you want it; it's coming if you don't.*"' I quoted without thinking.

Janine nodded. 'Precisely. Do you know what that means?'

I shook my head.

"You already know the aim of these experiments: to eliminate emotional weaknesses. But why? I'll tell you why: because they need soldiers, war machines with the ability to think divergently. Only emotion can make you a hindrance. It can make you disobedient. They don't want you to have morals. A few of us slip through the cracks and we're forced to be Ospreys. The rest are training.'

'Training?'

'To kill.'

My eyes widened. 'What did they take from you?'

'My apathy. I was floating around, not caring whether I lived or died, but they made me aware, stuck in this purgatory of sympathy. They stole my name. They stole my life. They created the perfect circumstances for me to die. My parents buried an empty casket.' She hung her head and began to whimper.

'So, who are you?'

'My name's Octavia Orville and I was just like you.' She took off her mask to reveal a face. Human, like mine. She had a nose she'd probably inherited from her father and eyes most likely from her mother. She'd lived.

She looked around frantically. 'Don't tell anyone what I've told you here. Whatever you do, don't give them any reason to punish you. We're legally dead and that means killing us isn't murder. Don't let them—'

Before she had time to finish her sentence, a loud, ceramic-sounding bell rattled the room.

'What shouldn't I let them?'

'I'm sorry, but you need to leave. GO. Quick. They're coming!'

'Who—'

A door at the back of the room burst open. Through it entered two big, burly cloaked bodies with beaks, looking like plague doctors from the Middle Ages if they'd had access to modern-day glamour and opalescent jewels. I assumed they were Vultures because of two things: a) I'd never seen them before, and b) they seemed to be a lot bigger and scarier than the Ospreys or even the one Buzzard I'd encountered.

'TIME IS UP, OCTAVIA!' said one of the Vultures with a completely accent-less voice. It was almost impossible to discern anything about the people behind those masks except that they weren't there to do good.

'GO!' screamed Octavia. She slapped my cheek lightly with her limp hand.

I leapt up from my crouching position and sprung towards the door before the Vultures had the chance to register my presence or my absence.

Outside, Galatea was waiting for me, hands deep in the pockets of her green low-waisted jeans. She was leaning against the wall, trying to look as nonchalant as possible, but I could tell she was buzzing with anxious and inquisitive energy on the inside.

As I turned towards her, her eyes widened, and she blinked a few times as if in disbelief.

'What happened in there? I heard a lot of shouting.'

'Stuff.'

'What did we talk about yesterday?' she asked in a patronising tone.

'I know, but…' I thought about it for a while. Octavia told me not to tell anyone. "I'm just confident that we're doing the right thing," I responded.

'Oookay…I have a feeling you're not gonna explain yourself, so why don't we discuss the N-A-L-P.'

'Am I dyslexic, or did you not just spell a word?'

'You're proper stupid.'

'Oh, I get it now! NO. This space is D-E-S-I-M-O-R-P-M-O-C,' I replied, winking in a deliberately corny way.

'Not even going to try.'

I rolled my eyes.

We walked out into the courtyard, and I explained my plan to her.

'So…what? Lemme play this back for you: you want Little Miss Russia to go all psycho-hyper and distract everyone while you, I, the emo and your chav girlfriend sneak out of the hall, climb into some musty vent and crawl around aimlessly, hoping for an exit and trying not to get chopped up by some massive fan? That's your big escape plan?' she scoffed.

I was so genuinely offended by this attack on my plan that I forgot all about where we were going and where I'd been. 'Unless you have a better idea.'

'Maybe we don't do it in broad daylight.'

'But lunchtime is the only time we can be sure all the staff are in the same place. Also, they'd expect people to escape at night, so they probably have everything on maximum security.'

'You're over thinking everything. Just consider today as a trial and error. We can scope out the vents during the free period and then try again at night.'

She let her face curl into a sullen scowl. 'We need to be more serious, like what exactly is Punishment? I think we should attend the assembly or whatever to see what it'll be like when we slip up eventually, or in my case when I don't have you to do these things for me. If Punishment turns out to be a stupid lecture, we can focus our efforts more on the plan, okay?' she said, speeding up her walking pace to a steady stride.

I just sighed. Janine's voice—Octavia's voice— echoed in my head: *'We're legally dead, and that means killing us isn't murder.'* A chill ran down my spine.

I let her get to the other side of the courtyard before even considering catching up to her.

The Buzzard stood outside the assembly hall, using their arms to indicate where we should queue up. 'Kalmia, here,' they said, shaking their right arm. 'Orchid, here,' they said, shaking their left.

Galatea and I lined up on their right, behind Talia. We were at the very back of the line, and neither Brynhild nor Pygmalion were anywhere to be found. Aphrodite wasn't there, but that was nothing new. Sylvia's Gothic-looking friend, the one with the thick kohl eye make-up—Beckah, I think—stood fidgeting and tapping her left foot repetitively on the floor as she gazed into a small pocket mirror, correcting her eyeliner with a dirty, bitten fingernail.

The rest of Sylvia's friends were lined up in front of us, chatting nervously to each other, conversing with shallow laughter and strained smiles, except for the boy with sun-dyed brown hair. Trish was what Sylvia had called him. No, he stood rocking back and forth on his heels, scratching his neck uncontrollably like someone suffering from withdrawal symptoms. His bloodshot eyes caught mine for a second, so I looked away, trying not to seem concerned.

Would Punishment reveal everything, or would it just add to my curiosity?

Well, at least *I* wasn't being punished.

The Buzzard produced a silver pocketwatch from seemingly nowhere and exclaimed, 'Well, I guess you can go in now. What a brief waiting period!'

They giggled as the murmur of the small crowd ceased, making way for the low crackling of the stagnant air that followed.

The doors opened behind them, absorbing the faint light from the atrium into an all-consuming void. Our line began to move forward in slow, lurching movements, like a human worm.

My feet moved as though they weren't under the control of my mind, thrusting me into the blackness with full force as, again, we were led into the theatre.

I took my seat in the second row, just in front of the stage. I placed my arms on the armrest to my left because the one on the right was obviously not mine.

As always, the lights switched on abruptly, their pugnacious beams pulling sweat from my pores, forcing it to drip down my nose. The curtains rose while we were still sitting in absolute darkness. Without the inner stage lights, the platform seemed to have been split into three sections, like a theatre stage; the floor made of scratched and polished dark oak wood. It was empty, devoid of anything but scaffolding, the bare bones of a set, and the usual microphone, planted firmly, front and centre, ready to be used by whoever happened to walk on the stage.

Talia turned and started to say something before stopping dead in her tracks. 'I think this whole thing is—oh…you're not Galatea,' she said.

'It appears so.'

'I saw her here like two seconds ago. Who are you?'

'Samson.' I yawned.

'Can we be friends?'

'Maybe. Do you have any useful information about anything? It doesn't matter how mund—'

'Shut up—Madame H is coming!'

I snapped my attention back to the stage. So, she was.

She walked on, free from her usual proud demeanour, face full of cakey makeup, legs thick and with a fake orange tan. Her look was completed by a droopy red smile and garish and crass eyeliner. She licked her lips and cleared her throat. At that moment, she resembled a very orange lizard.

'Hello, children. As much as I regret hosting this assembly, it is mandatory, and it is fully deserved. I had given you full warning of the consequences of your actions, of breaking the rules, but most of you seem to have decided you're too good for the rules. Well, you aren't, though I suppose you are less mature than adults, and your hormone-addled, half-baked frontal lobes give you the stupid compulsion to do the opposite of what you've been told. I mean, God forbid I let you off the hook, but I'll give you one more chance,' she rambled, waving her hand about.

'I'll show you what happens when you test my goodwill.' Madame H coughed and pointed to stage left.

'BRING HER OUT!' she shouted to the people waiting in the wings.

The lights flickered and dimmed, shifting when something emerged from the wings. On rolled some squeaky piece of hospital apparatus covered in brown poison ivy, thick crimson rust and dried bodily fluids. As the old metal gurney was thrust onto the stage, the varnished floor creaked beneath it as if unprepared to bear its weight. When the gurney reached centre stage, Madame Hortense strutted off, her face portraying something completely adverse to her body language.

On one end of the gurney was the Buzzard, and on the other was another run-of-the-mill Osprey. The Osprey wrapped a slack cord around an object on the gurney and tied it with a pained groan coming from the lump. The object was long, human-shaped and covered in a white sheet. The rest of the cord disappeared from its post on the side of the gurney as it was pulled offstage by someone in the wings. The thing writhed and screeched until the Buzzard punched it hard in what was probably its stomach.

When the rope was secure, the Buzzard took a knife and slit the sheet wide open.

Offstage helpers hoisted the thing up by the cord around its waist, putting it on display for all to see. The sheet fell away, stained with fresh and old blood. Above us was somebody I knew.

I didn't know her well.

I didn't know her at all.

Little Octavia Orville.

My heart jumped into my throat, almost exactly where they'd stitched hers.

Her arms were spread as if nailed to some invisible crucifix.

I lurched forward, vomit burning my oesophagus.

From the distance we were at, the putrescent stench of her exposed innards burned my nose. They had been stitched lackadaisically to her peeling skin, her lungs tied around her neck like an undulating flesh necklace, and her heart still pumping blood through the tree trunk veins and arteries that now ran over her skin rather than under it in a cacophony of red and blue branches, yanked clean from their moorings.

I'd never seen anything so awful in my entire life; not even the execution videos or chain mail I'd been sent were sick enough to even come close to this.

I had no idea how they'd been able to turn her inside out in under two hours, but nonetheless, I was horrified.

The creaks and huffs of the synthetic metal pipes making up for the carefully created tubes of the natural human body bore into my skull with so much blunt force it could've given me a TBI.

My eyes watered, rendering everything blurry. My body tensed with its efforts not to vomit up my organs and trying not to cry.

It hit me then: we had to leave.

NOW.

The worst thing about it was that she was still alive. Her eyes flickered intermittently, revealing her darkened sclera.

The other Osprey gestured to the Buzzard, making very aggressive hand movements. In a random twitch, one of Octavia's fractured legs kicked the Osprey in the face, pushing back her hood.

Her skin was a jaundiced type of brown that reminded me of early morning skies in smog-filled cities. She looked dangerously pale…dead, even.

Although my vision was blurry, I could see her jet-black Bantu knots and the remainder of her hair curling around her neck, snaking down to rest upon her clavicle.

Like Octavia, she had a white mask resembling a bird. Unlike Octavia, hers had massive eye sockets and an ivory-white complexion with a visible bone-smooth texture. The beak covered her nose, fragile and almost sheer, like a real beak.

She looked down at the audience with disdain.

My gaze wandered up to her face, trying to get a better look.

Her eyes met mine.

It couldn't be.

It wasn't.

It shouldn't be.

But it had to be.

My lips moved, mouthing a word I'd dreaded to say since last October: 'Samantha.'

I didn't kill her.

There was no relief in that sentence.

I didn't kill her.

But I really should have.

Beside me, Galatea gasped deep and hard as if she were emerging from icy water.

I leaned back in my seat and turned my head to face her so I wouldn't puke.

She gripped my face with her calloused fingers and pulled me close, eyes wide and teeth chattering, 'We're leaving. TONIGHT,' she declared between gags and shallow breaths.

I nodded and looked to my other side. Talia wasn't there.

I had no time to waste looking for her.

I grabbed Galatea and dragged her with me as I walked calmly toward the exit. I looked at the rows of people in nail-biting silence. The air was thick with sickness, decay, blood and screams enough to curdle it.

Astoundingly, there was no one at the doors to make sure we didn't leave, and I burst through them, my lungs embracing the scent and feel of the fresh air.

I basically leapt up the stairs, sweat soaking the base of my neck. My knees creaked and ached as I reached the landing, my socks muffling my footsteps. I flung open the door to our room, and just as quickly slammed it shut after Galatea rushed through.

Brynhild was sitting cross-legged on her bed, talking to some sort of Raggedy Anne-esque doll with a dazed look in her wide brown eyes. Her glasses were askew on the floor, scratched and laying lens side down as if they'd been thrown across the room in some sort of fit.

Pygmalion was sitting on the floor beside a large stack of thick, leather-bound books with one of them stuck under his nose, held up by hands the colour of teeth and as skinny as fallen autumn twigs. He had the same glassy-eyed look.

I listened to the ambience of the room, of which there wasn't any. The only things I could hear were my heart's pounding beats and the sound of Galatea's heavy breathing, cloaked only by my own.

Pygmalion sat right at the foot of my bed, slouched over the old, dusty tome, flicking sluggishly through the time-beaten pages. He was moving, but so slowly, that I couldn't recognise his movements as being human.

I crossed the room as quietly as possible, trying not to disturb the pair in their dazed mindlessness. I stole past Pygmalion and searched my bed, flipping the saliva-stained pillow off of it before grabbing the package there and holding it. I took a peek at Pygmalion's book: every single page was blank. I held the package up to show Galatea.

'What even is that?' she wheezed at full volume, breathless from the run upstairs.

I beckoned her with my left hand.

Galatea crept over, making only a slight effort to conceal her stomping footfalls, and leaned in to see the contents wrapped in the musty shower curtain. I tilted my hand slightly forward, displaying the gleaming screws and rusty nails, along with the paper clips, Kirby grips and toothbrush.

The sharpened blue toothbrush.

Next to us, Brynhild jerked, her entire body twitching for just a split second.

Galatea rummaged through the sharp objects. Clearly, they were satisfactory, as she looked up at me and nodded. I hopped onto the bed and began to unscrew the vent above it, using the rusty screws Sylvia had given me. I gave Galatea a lift up, and she started to help me.

Then, out of the blue, the room door flung open so violently that the door handle dented the plaster on impact. In the doorway stood the very person who'd inspired my plan, looking rather unsightly. Her hair was matted with clumps of something thick and red, her skin dotted with matching cardinal splatters. She leaned against the door frame, leaving a red mark behind her when she moved.

'Why are you covered in blood?' Galatea asked, voicing my query.

'Listen, I've put up with your BS for long enough. Can we, like…not?'

'Oh, Aphrodite, we're a bit busy here…come back later?' I suggested, wincing slightly in preparation for her response.

Once again, she put her middle finger up at me.

'Oh, grow up. It's just a finger,' Galatea groaned, presumably at Aphrodite.

'Whatever you're doing, I want in—'

'No.' I stopped unscrewing and crossed my arms, glaring at her.

'But—'

'No.'

'But—'

'Jesus Christ, close the door,' I requested, pinching the bridge of my nose. It actually hurt quite a lot.

Aphrodite stepped inside and closed the door behind her.

'Almost got it. What was supposed to happen was you walking out of the room first and then closing the door with you on the other side.' I glared at her.

'Want to try again?' Galatea chimed in, cocking her head in a mimicking sort of way.

'Why are you so mean?' Aphrodite said.

'What are you talking about? I don't know you, and you don't know me, so don't act like you do.' I leered at her.

The hematic girl looked up at me with eyes like saucers, trying to find a witty retort.

My first screw fell out of the vent covering. Galatea was also done with hers.

'Don't you want help?' Aphrodite shouted in desperation, waving her water-wrinkled, imbrued hands around.

'No.'

She surveyed the room frantically, whipping her head from side to side as her damp hair slapped her neck, leaving blood splatters on her neck.

I resumed my efforts to remove the screws.

Aphrodite strode over to Brynhild, tore the doll from her hands and waited for a reaction.

'Don't you want to know where Brynhild found this stupid doll or where the books are coming from? Don't you have any questions whatsoever?' Aphrodite yelled, spinning around to face me.

My second screw fell out into the palm of my hand. Galatea had been done with hers for a while. I threaded my fingers through the grate and tried to dislodge it from the wall, tapping Galatea, who was wrapping up the bundle of sharp objects, on the shoulder.

She copied me and started to pull. With our combined strength, we managed to yank the vent grate from its place in the canvas wallpaper. It fell and landed on the bed with a soft thud.

I turned to Aphrodite. 'No, I think we'll be just fine.' I smirked.

Galatea gripped the inside of the vent shaft and hoisted herself up, using the headboard of my bed as a sort of stepping stone.

Aphrodite dropped the doll and ran her fingers through her hair, coating them with congealed blood and crystalised hair gel. She found her roots, gripped them tightly, and jumped up and down like a spoiled brat who didn't get her way.

She shrieked something unintelligible and high-pitched, something along the lines of 'THIS ISN'T HOW IT GOES!' and 'I'VE DONE NOTHING, GOD!'

When all I could see of Galatea washer dirty socks, I followed suit and clambered in, but before I did, I waved to Aphrodite. 'Have a nice life,' I said with a chuckle.

16

I crawled through the vent, shuffling forward with my forearms.

As exciting as an escape was, I could not ignore the sores forming on my elbows.

The vent looked exactly how you'd expect a vent to look: dark, metal and filled with cobwebs. Occasionally, I'd hear the odd scrabbling of murine feet or the spinning of a fan, but that was it.

I thought that now that we were alone for an indefinite period of time, it was the perfect time to have a conversation with Galatea.

'So…do you have any hobbies?' I said, talking to her dirty, sweaty socks because I obviously couldn't see her face.

'WHAT?' she looked back at me and shouted.

'DO YOU HAVE ANY HOBBIES?' I nearly screamed back.

'Jeez, Louise, no need to yell!'

I rolled my eyes in the dark. 'So, do you?' I repeated.

'You're really boring, you know that?'

'What do you mean?' I said, feigning shock.

'*Do you have any hobbies?* I mean, next, you'll be asking me what my favourite shape is!'

'How would you start a conversation, Little Miss Chatterbox? I didn't hear you networking during French,' I said with a huff.

'Okay...valid,' she agreed. 'So...hobbies?'

'Yes.'

'Well, I'm your average dream girl.' She giggled sarcastically. 'I live a normal life: I sew, I pretend to read novels, I try to do calligraphy, and I sometimes kickbox.'

'One of those things is not like the others—does that mean you could absolutely wipe the floor with me?'

'NO! I'd never hurt someone unnecessarily. I opened up to you, and this is what I get?'

'Okay, okay—carry on.'

'I don't want to anymore. Let's hear about your hobbies.'

I looked behind me and could still faintly see the light of the room we'd just left. 'I will, but can we move a little faster first, please?'

Galatea shuffled a little bit faster. Not much, but it was enough.

'I don't really have any hobbies.'

'I didn't think you would. It's a boring conversation starter, anyway. At this point, I'll even take MSN as a hobby. Anything as long as it's not scrolling through Reddit or 4chan.' She sighed.

'What's 4chan?' I asked, feigning innocence. I hoped she didn't notice.

'Never mind.'

We crawled a bit farther until the floor of the ventilation tunnel was illuminated by some type of light underneath it, peeking through the open grates below.

I stopped suddenly, but Galatea continued.

The room beneath the vent tube was the one where they'd injected us. It looked unnaturally dark now that the inconspicuous windows were covered with blackout blinds, and the only source of light was the glow of the numerous screens around the room. The light was somewhat eerie, an uncanny shade of aqua that subsumed the face of the only person inside the room.

From the rough silhouette visible from my point of view, it looked rather like Madame Hortense, only she didn't have her business jacket on, and her arms were enveloped by blue, elbow-length surgical gloves. She was also wearing a very obviously fake pearl necklace.

That was new.

She was hunched over a desk with a couple of red vials in front of her. Behind the vials was what looked like a microscope. She spun around to retrieve something from a nearby work surface.

I strained my eyes—it looked a bit like a packet of cotton swabs.

She slid one gently out of the package and swabbed the insides of both of her cheeks six times before removing it. After that, I couldn't really see what was going on as she had her back to the vent.

I looked away from the room and struggled in the darkness for a minute until I saw Galatea, who had made considerable progress.

I used my clammy palms to stick to the sides of the vent so I could push myself forward as I tried to catch up. 'I did not think this through,' I admitted as I gazed into the endless metallic intestines of the building.

'I know you didn't, but there is literally no turning back now. The only way is onward,' Galatea said, strangely calm after I'd confessed that we were wandering around blindly.

'It'll be okay. You got us a way out of the room. That's more than I could ever hope for on my own.'

The tunnel's heavy silence echoed in my brain.

'You're a good person: I hope you know that.' I sighed and reached out to touch her foot in a weird show of affection.

'I'm glad *you* think that.' Her voice, filled with a strange type of sorrow, reverberated in the confined space. It was almost as if her cry for help was muffled by others' expectations and rolled up in a glue trap.

'I don't know how I wouldn't think that. You've been nothing but nice to me since I met you, and the only thing that's changed is the situation. I think you *deserve* to make it out of here.'

My chest swelled as I spoke, and something overcame me. It was a mix of pity and understanding, but it felt like something entirely new. I was feeling an emotion that didn't exist, and it felt like bleeding.

'You're only human, after all.'

'Apparently, being only human isn't good enough,' Galatea said with a sigh.

Somehow, we made it to the other end of the vent labyrinth. Galatea peered out of the holes in the rust-covered vent grate.

'So, what do you see?' I asked from behind her.

'Well, it's night, and there's grass below us. Lots of grass. In fact, we're mostly surrounded by grass. As far as I can see, it's a flat, barren terrain. If they have lookout posts, they'll spot us almost instantly.'

'How far up from the ground are we?'

'Hard to say. About a two-storey drop, but it might be more. I can't really tell because it's dark.'

'So, what do we do now?' I asked. There was a serpent writhing in my stomach, telling me that we were completely and utterly stuck.

'Move back,' Galatea commanded.

'What?' I asked, shuffling backwards.

'Move back!' she repeated as she sat up and flipped her legs forward so she was lying on her back with her knees bent, feet right up against the rusty vent covering.

'What are you doing?' I asked as she began kicking the vent loose.

'You're a smart boy, Samson—hazard a guess.'

Her foot was assaulted by bits of rusty metal as it crashed through the grate. Blood pooled in the toe of her sock. She pushed her legs through the hole, biting her lip as the jagged fragments of the vent cover threatened to peel the skin off of her thighs. I heard it when her legs bashed against the wall.

'How're you going to get down?'

'This wall feels like cobblestone. The bricks are massive,' she responded, sliding her body farther.

'That doesn't answer my question.'

She pushed her head through before gripping the upper part of the covering.

'I'll just figure it o—OHMYGOD!'

I grabbed onto her sweaty hands before I could even stop to think.

If you let go—

If you let go, I'll never let you forgive yourself.

She appeared to have lost her balance and was now hanging by her arms, her legs dangling below her. I gazed at her from above. Her skin was pure white where the metal had cut it.

The red spilt from her flayed tissue, and it practically felt as if the lacerations had been applied to my own body as if my own skin had been torn and mangled by the rust.

Her face was twisted by the darkness as she looked up at me.

'I can try to pull you–'

'NO.'

WHAT DO YOU MEAN, 'NO'?

Her eyes shimmered like earthbound stars.

'What? Why?' My trembling hands gripped hers as she squirmed, trying to escape.

'I'm not going back. I'm not a lab rat,' said Galatea.

I didn't know how to react to that. Although it wasn't intended for me, the coldness of her voice drenched my body in sweat. 'What do you mean?'

I felt tears wetting my eyes.

I didn't want to cry.

I didn't have to cry.

What would she think of me if I started crying?

'We've come this far.'

'Yeah, I know, but where will we go when we get out? How are we ever going to survive out there, where there are thieves and opportunists who'd kill us just because they could?' I pleaded with her.

'In here, they'll kill us anyway.'

'I think we need to know what's up here before we leave everyone. We have a way out, but when we get back to the real world, who's going to believe us? We need proof. We need to know exactly what's happening.'

Coursing through me was this earth-shattering feeling that tore right through my body, disrupting the very structure of my being and destroying the order of how everything should and would be.

I held her tighter.

It was so awful, but not like an axe to the heart or any other sappy metaphor. It was a rent straight down the middle of me, letting every good or happy thought seep out of me like blood from a deep gash.

'Why can't you just let me go?' She looked over her shoulder and bit her lip.

'WE CAN'T LEAVE YET.' My voice cracked as I shouted at her through the violent wind picking up outside.

'Who's to stop me?' she whispered with a suspicious glint in her eye, and she let go of my hands.

NO.

NO.

NO.

NO.

NO.

NO.

NO.

My organs plaited themselves into a noose around my skeleton, hanging it over and over again. Seeing her fall was like shoving razor blades into every orifice. My fingers curled as I gasped for air that'd be better off not coming.

NO.

NO.

NO.

NO.

NO.

NO.

NO.

The tears in my eyes fell onto the protruding cobblestones. As they fell, a thousand petawatts of electricity cramped up my legs and raced through my bloodstream.

Every twitch felt like a slur branded into my flesh, like the mark of Cain.

NO.

NO.

NO.

NO.

NO.

NO.

NO!

Her nails made an awful sort of grating noise as she slid down the wall.

My mind raced.

You can't just let her go!

You'll never make the journey back.

What if something happens to her?

I looked behind me at the long, winding maze of tunnels. Then I peered down at the drop.

DO IT!

I wanted to jump, but what were the consequences?

DO IT!

I mean, I couldn't just let her go alone…

DO IT!

But my sister was here—shouldn't I finish the job? Shouldn't I justify my guilt? Shouldn't I make her pay for the worst year of my life?

DO IT!

And what kind of person would I be if I left Sylvia here, high and dry?

DO IT!

I could talk myself out of it all I wanted, but in the end, I knew I was going to—

DO IT!

Oftentimes, when stuck between a rock and a hard place, it's the obvious choice to take the easiest way out. This time, the easiest way was down.

ABOUT THE AUTHOR

Gyeni Goman is a 13-year-old writer with a deep passion for storytelling and a love of reading. Her debut novel, 'A Flightless Bird›, has evolved through various unfinished iterations over the years, and she is thrilled to share it in its completed form.

Currently, Gyeni is busy working on her next book and has even considered a sequel to her first. In addition to writing, she enjoys drawing and illustrating, adding her unique touch to her creative projects.

Transforming diverse writers
into successful published authors

www.consciousdreamspublishing.com

authors@consciousdreamspublishing.com

Let's connect